Harlequin's Collection

A reprint series of fondly remembered
Harlequin Romances

SUSAN BARRIE

The Stars of San Cecilio

Originally published as Harlequin Romance #730

CRAIG

Harlequin Books

TORONTO · LONDON · NEW YORK · AMSTERDAM · SYDNEY · WINNIPEG

Original hard cover edition published by Mills & Boon Limited

SBN 373-00730-2

Harlequin edition published April 1963

This *Harlequin's Collection* edition printed 1976

LISA looked at herself critically in the mirror. Then she smiled a little sadly, because she was looking her best— and it was her last night in San Cecilio!

Her frock, with the huge scarlet poppies surrounding the hem, was new and as yet unworn. The main part of it was plain ivory taffeta and against it her tanned arms and shoulders had the pale hue of apricots. Her hair formed bright wings of gold falling to her shoulders, and her eyes had a shy look about them, and were grey as wood smoke. She had used rather more lipstick than she normally did, and her lips looked soft, eager and — hopeful?

She sighed as she remembered that it *was* her last night in San Cecilio, and last nights—when a whole thirteen had gone before without anything to distinguish their passing—seldom provided anything memorable. And even if it did it would be in the nature of an anti-climax, for this time tomorrow night Spain would belong entirely to her past.

She went to the window and looked out at the stars that were hanging above the sleeping sea. They were such huge stars that she felt her breath catch with wonder as she looked up at them. Like lamps, she thought dreamily — like lamps suspended by invisible threads; and where each one peered at itself in the indigo waste of waters there was a shimmer like phosphorescence. The same white light made the beach look curving and ghostly, and the strangely-shaped rocks that littered the beach were like monsters crouching out there in the gloom.

Inland the coast swung away into dim distance, scattered with lights like a string of pearls. They were the lights of hotels, the lights of villas crowning the slopes, the riding-lights of the odd yacht anchored here and there. And in that gentle darkness before the moon rose there was the breathless scent of flowers that blazed in every garden in San Cecilio in the daytime.

Lisa moved back to the dressing-table and added a final flick of powder to her nose. She dabbed perfume behind her ears, and fastened a small pendant on a neat platinum chain about her neck.

What did it matter, she thought, if such sweetness as she possessed was about to be wasted on the desert air of a hotel dining-room? This last night she would order a bottle of Vino de Champaña, sample one or two dishes that she had been afraid to sample hitherto, and absorb as many last night impressions as she possibly could to take back with her to England at the close of the one and only holiday on foreign soil that she had ever enjoyed in her life.

And even now she couldn't say whether she had enjoyed it or not.

As she was wafted downwards in the lift she knew what would await her in the dining-room. There would be the orchestra, composed chiefly of guitars, playing away softly, but with Spanish zest, against a background of palms and flower-wreathed pillars. Outside the wide-flung windows there would be the lazy slap and murmur of the sea; inside, the popping of champagne corks, the laughter of women. Most of the women would wear lovely dresses—far lovelier than her simple cream taffeta with the hand-painted poppies on the skirt—and fabulous jewellery, and the men would all have acquired that added distinction bestowed by evening dress. Some would wear white shell-jackets and cummerbunds, which she thought more attractive than the regulation evening kit. And as it was Spain, most of the men would have sleek black hair, like patent leather under the lights, and they would smoke cigars with their coffee and liqueurs.

There would be the man with the blackest hair she had ever seen in her life—or, at least, she hoped he would be there again this evening!—seated at a table placed discreetly in an alcove, his thin, dark, thoughtful face bent above a newspaper, or a book, which he would have brought with him to the meal. Never once had he looked across at Lisa while they were in the same room together, although her eyes had dwelt on him often. There was an air of imperviousness, of remoteness, about him that was like a protective cloak, shielding him from even the thought of intrusion, or the knowledge of his surroundings.

The waiters who watched over him with extra attentiveness never broke through his wall of abstraction. He had beautiful, long-fingered hands that looked dark and strong against the pages of his book, and his face in that perpetual repose was beautiful also—like the faces of medieval knights in early prints, or stained-glass windows.

Only on one occasion had Lisa seen him dining with anybody, and that was a ravishing woman of about thirty, with hair that seemed to flame, although she wore it in orderly plaits about a regally poised head. Her eyes were like mysterious black velvet, her throat had a magnolia whiteness, and diamonds sparkled like water at her ears, and about that same white throat. She had an air of composure that matched her companion's aloofness, and throughout the meal neither of them laughed, or appeared in the slightest degree gay; although to any ordinary onlooker they were very content.

Afterwards, although it was a gala night, they had not joined in the dancing on the smooth ballroom floor, but had sat on the terrace with a bottle of wine on the little table between them, and dishes of salted almonds and olives.

The night had been heady with the scent of the pines that enclosed San Cecilio, and the perfume of the countless flowers hidden in the dusk. And the woman had worn a golden dress that gleamed like the scaly skin of a serpent, and her lips might have been lacquered scarlet, and in addition to the mystery in her eyes there had been a suggestion of repletion—of no more seeking!

On another occasion this man of thirty-five, or thereabouts, who was obviously a native of the country, had shared his table at lunch with a small, plain, jetty-haired girl, and a very English-looking nannie, whose voice had carried clearly to Lisa. She had been complaining in English because her charge had defied her about something, and instead of looking repentant the charge had giggled defiantly. Lisa had felt extraordinarily drawn towards her, and the impishness that dwelt in her enormous long-lashed eyes, her only redeeming feature.

But tonight, as she passed between the swing doors into the main restaurant, she had the feeling that the thin-faced man might not be there at his table. And she was right. There was no one else at his table, and it was plainly waiting for him, but while Lisa ploughed through several courses without any appetite whatsoever the table remained like an island of loneliness, decorated with wine-dark carnations, but otherwise deserted.

After dinner Lisa felt as if the one thing she had looked forward to all day had disappointed her, and now there was no longer any hope. Any hope of what? she asked herself, as she made her way out into the warm, soft, enfolding darkness of the night.

She couldn't—or wouldn't—answer; but her disappointment was acute. She even felt as if there was a lump in her throat that made it ache slightly as she leaned against the parapet of the terrace, and watched couples moving down there in the rich gloom of the garden. The haunting, incessant thrumming of guitars reached her, the couples were all obviously of one mind, and that was to find some spot where no one was likely to burst rudely upon them, or interfere with the magic of their evening, and only Lisa seemed to have no one at all to speak to, or with any ardent desire for her company.

She moved away down the terrace steps, feeling acutely self-conscious because of her aloneness. It wasn't that she was unsociable or that she found it difficult to make friends easily. But she had so little money to spend during this holiday, and she had kept herself to herself. She had realized at the outset that if she had allowed herself to be drawn into parties she would inevitably spend more than she could afford, and somehow she was not the type to whom gay male escorts attached themselves. She was shy, and she looked on the defensive, wary even. Masculine eyes admired her and her bright wings of hair, her fragile, "little-girl" figure, the aura of primness that made her seem rather quaint, but they left her alone. Perhaps they thought she was the type it was safest to leave alone, because her eyes were serious, and seriousness and a holiday spirit seldom go well together.

And, for her part, Lisa was not even aware of the admiring masculine looks. Since her arrival in San Cecilio she had been aware only of one dark masculine head, and eyes that never looked towards her, but which she knew were dark also. A dark head and eyes that were as far removed from her as the stars!

As she walked down the flower-banked drive she thought with an agonized feeling of resentment that Fate might have been kind, and let her see him for the last time! Wasn't it enough that

9

she had to go back to England without even a job to return to, because Mrs. Hamilton-Tracey had picked that quarrel with her over the children's bath-water? There had been nothing wrong with the children's bath-water. The temperature had been absolutely right, as it always was, and the fact that Roddy turned the hot tap on just as his mother looked in after returning hot and frustrated from a trip to London had been most unfortunate. Roddy had screamed that he was being scalded, and Ann had scampered about the bathroom, delighting in the din, and shrieked that she had been scalded, too, when the water was "boiling", as she described it! Mrs. Hamilton-Tracey had rushed furiously to the cold tap and turned it on, and then had snatched her son out of the water and declared that she had never heard of anything so disgraceful.

Roddy had hugged her closely with his wet arms, and the expensive grosgrain suit she was wearing had been ruined. So had the organdie frills of her white blouse, and the suede shoes into which Roddy had dripped bath water. Lisa had labored over the suit afterwards, but not even her skilful pressing had restored its earlier beauty, and it had had to be sent away to the cleaners.

And then one thing had led to another, and Lisa had discovered that she was expected to act as lady's maid as well as children's governess (or nannie, as she actually was,) and Mrs. Hamilton-Tracey had brought to light piles of her underwear that she declared had been neglected. Lisa had never understood that it was her job to mend nylon stockings, lift and lower hemlines, obliterate cigarete burns in evening dresses, as well as attend to all the children's clothes. She had been with the Hamilton-Traceys for over a year, but these late duties had only just been outlined to her.

She realized that Mrs. Hamilton-Tracey wanted to be rid of her. Mr. Hamilton-Tracey had been kind — a weakness that was foreign to Mrs. Hamilton-Tracey's nature — and his wife had resented it. She had very little use for him, but consideration for an employee had aroused her ire—it was just possbile her jealousy.

So, on the very eave of leaving for her holiday, having saved up carefully for it, Lisa found herself bereft of a job.

Of course, no doubt she would soon find another when she got back. There were so many children in the world, and in spite of the derogatory reference she might receive from Mrs. Hamilton-Tracey she was born to look after children. She loved them, and they loved her—even the impish Roddy, who had wept himself sick when he made the discovery that once she went away she was never likely to return.

She passed between the ornamental wrought-iron gates of the hotel, and stood on San Cecilio's cobbled main highway. Cars whizzed past her in the lights that streamed from the hotel; they were long and streamlined and mostly pastel-colored, like Devonshire clotted cream and light sky blue. They glittered with chromium, and she saw how festive and relaxed the occupants of them appeared, lying back against contrasting upholstery.

In front of her the sea whispered, and from the Plaza on one side of her came the gay note of accordions, and laughing voices. She knew that if she joined those laughing voices she would look out of place, an English girl with strikingly English hair amongst dark-eyed Spaniards, and girls who still wore mantillas, and were ready to snatch roses from behind their ears and toss them when the moment seemed ripe.

No, for her the sea definitely beckoned, and she went down to it and the little jetty at the foot of which the gentle wavelets lapped. She still felt like someone with a grievance—someone who wanted to cry because Fate *had* been unkind, and this was her last night—and indeed she felt like the beggar-maid who had dared to lift her eyes to King Cophetua. Only for a fortnight the king hadn't noticed that she was there crouching at his feet, just waiting for one little crumb of notice to be flung at her.

She stood leaning against the rail of the jetty and felt ashamed of herself because even to herself she couldn't pretend. She was twenty-four, and she had never been in love with any man, but in future she was never going to get away from the remembrance of one man who wasn't even of her own nationality, and certainly didn't belong to her world. He belonged to the world of expensive hotels and deferential waiters, diamond-decked women and little girls who were looked after by well-trained English nannies who wore trim uniforms.

English nannies! . . .

A dizzy thought leapt through her mind, and she watched the moon rise and climb slowly above the sea as if it was a huge golden lantern someone was swinging aloft. And then when the moon was no longer golden, but clear and pale and shedding a primrose light across the wide path of the ocean, she turned away, only to make the discovery that the high heel of one of her evening slippers had caught between the cobbles of the jetty.

She wrenched at it, but nothing happened. She removed her foot from the shoe and bent down to try to twist it free; but still nothing happened, and she was beginning to despair and wonder what it would feel like hobbling back up the drive to her hotel with only one shoe and a stockinged foot, when a man who had been sauntering along the waterfront and thoughtfully smoking a cigarette realized that she was in difficulties and crossed to her assistance.

"Your pardon, *señorita*!" he said, very quietly, and then bent and quickly released the shoe for her. He handed it back, looking at her with grave dark eyes. "It would have been uncomfortable to walk without it," he added, but all she could do was stare at him.

"Yes," she said—"Oh, yes!" And then wondered whether this was an hallucination, or whether Fate had really relented at last.

"Don't you think it would be a good idea if you put it on?" he suggested, and the smile on his beautifully cut lips was very slight.

But as she still stood with the shoe in her hands he removed it from her and himself bent and attached the pale satin sandal to the slim foot to which it belonged. Then he straightened and looked down at her from a height that was several inches above her own, and there was something quizzical in his regard.

"I should have done that in the beginning, shouldn't I?" he remarked. "Although it was Cinderella who lost her slipper, and there is nothing about you that suggests a Cinderella!"

CHAPTER TWO

LISA was so convinced that this was all part of wishful thinking that for several seconds her brain refused to tick over normally, and she stood staring up at him with a look in her large, shadowy grey eyes that would have flattered him excessively if he had had any clue to what lay behind that look. But it was obvious that he hadn't, and his eyebrows contracted suddenly in a puzzled fashion.

"Haven't I seen you before?" he asked. "I feel sure that I have."

Lisa swallowed something in her throat. It was a queer, excited dryness.

"Yes," she answered. "We are staying at the same hotel."

"The Carabela?"

"Yes."

This time his eyebrows ascended.

"Then I must have noticed you in the restaurant, or on the terrace. I don't frequent the hotel grounds very much, and I never visit the beach—at any rate, not in the daytime—so it was very probably the restaurant. You are staying in San Cecilio, *señorita*?"

"I've just concluded a fortnight's stay here," she admitted, her heart beating fast because, after all, he *had* noticed her. "And," she added, with infinite regret, "I go home tomorrow!"

He smiled.

"You sound sad, *señorita*—is it because you have fallen in love with San Cecilio? Many English people find the Costa Brava attractive, and you are quite obviously very English."

"Am I?"

His eyes flickered over her with that cool, faint smile in them.

14

"Yes—very!"

He turned, and she found herself walking at his side along the moon-bathed waterfront. He was wearing a white dinner-jacket, and her charmed eyes had already observed that he had a flower stuck in the lapel, a wine-dark carnation that filled the air with a rich aroma even as they walked. There was also the choice aroma of cigar-smoke adhering to him, and the beautifully masculine odor of shaving-cream; and as she peeped at him sideways his face looked smooth and clear-cut as a plaque, and the night-darkness of his hair formed a slight Marie Stuart peak on his forehead.

"There is always a certain sadness about the word *adios*—good-bye," he said, in his faultless but faintly accented English. "To say good-bye to a spot where one has been happy, if only for a short time, is disturbing because there is so much finality about it. One knows that one can never recapture an experience exactly as it was, however hard one might try in future."

"Yes, but that applies to everything in life, doesn't it?" she suggested, talking up shyly, but with interest.

"I think it was one of your own poets—no, it was a Frenchman—who said that in each farewell one dies a little death," he remarked moodily, as they moved almost noiselessly side by side. Then he looked down at the golden hair swinging close to his shoulder, the outline of a pensive brow and firm but demure chin, and he smiled more naturally. "But for me, I live only in Madrid, and there is no need to die the death when I say farewell to the Costa Brava."

"You come here often?" she asked, a lump in her throat because every minute as it ticked away was bringing her nearer to her own moment of farewell, and by some irony these words he was uttering to her were being uttered on her last night. "Not so very often, but it is a pleasant escape from city life. And at that moment I am looking for a house."

"Oh—yes?" she said.

"A house for the summer—a villa where I can install my family."

"Oh, yes?" she said again, more faintly.

"My daughter and her English nurse."

It was on the tip of Lisa's tongue to ask: "And your wife?" But she hadn't the courage to let it pass her lips.

"It becomes very hot in Madrid as the season advances," he explained, "and here on the coast there is usually some air, and always of course the tonic effect of the sea breezes. My daughter is not particularly strong; in fact, it is not long since she was seriously ill, and it behooves me to get her away for the summer. Then, in the autumn, she can go to school in England as planned."

"In England?" she echoed. "You believe in English schools?"

"In this case, yes," he answered. "My wife was partly English."

Was partly English! . . . Lisa stared away over the sea, and the iridescent shimmer dazzled her eyes. He was a widower, and Fate was permitting her to know him for a single night!

"I think I saw your little girl the other day," she told him. "She was having lunch with you."

Suddenly he stopped, and his voice was full of apology.

"Your pardon, *señorita*, but I am talking to you of my affairs, and I have not had the good manners to introduce myself! My name is Julio Fernandez. I am more than happy that I came along in time to rescue your slipper from the tenacious grip of the jetty cobbles!"

16

If there was humor in his voice, there was also a smooth sincerity, and underneath the smoothness there was a touch of warmth that felt like warm fingers reaching and closing about Lisa's heart. She turned her face up to him with an eagerness that made her look enchantingly attractive in the moonlight, and as she impulsively thrust back the bright wings of hair from her shoulders she responded:

"And I am Lisa Waring—Elizabeth Waring. I'm sure I should have had to abandon my shoe if you hadn't come along."

"Instead of which it is once more safely attached to your foot." He looked down at the foot as if its small size intrigued him. "Are you in a hurry to get back to the hotel, Miss Waring? Or, since we have met, will you drink a glass of wine with me on this last night of yours in San Cecilio?"

For an instant Lisa could hardly believe her own ears, and then she almost gasped in pleasure.

"That would be—lovely!"

His eyes flickered over her once more, dark, inscrutable eyes that nevertheless had the lustre of pools hidden in the depths of a shadowy wood, into which two brilliant stars were peering.

"*Bueno!*" he exclaimed. "I am very happy! There is a *bodega* not far from here that will not be too crowded at this hour, and we will drink to your return to San Cecilio—if it is your wish that you should return here at some distant future date?"

"Not too far distant," she returend, a little shakily.

"Then some future date that is perhaps nearer than you imagine."

The *bodega* was not far from the quayside, and they had to retrace their steps to get to it. Inevitably music floated out through the open doorway, and a flood of mellow light fell across the rough

17

wooden benches and tables set out on the cool stone floor. Trailing vines and pot plants gave the place atmosphere.

In spite of the crudeness of the seating accommodation the wine, when it was brought to the table, was the finest Lisa had so far tasted. She realized that she was hardly a connoisseur of wines, but even her inexperienced palate detected a quality in this sparkling beverage that sent a pleased look into her eyes as she looked across the table at her escort. It was golden and glowing like ripe apricots, and as clear as glass, and as she looked down at the bubbles that floated in it she felt a trifle bemused.

"To your future happiness, Miss Waring," Julio Feranandez said formally. "To a great deal of good fortune in your future — and a return to San Cecilio!"

"I am not in the least likely to return to San Cecilio," Lisa confessed forlornly when she set down her glass.

"Why not?" he asked.

And although she couldn't understand afterwards why she decided all at once to be quite truthful and uninhibited about her affairs, she found herself telling him how she had saved up for this holiday, and about the disaster that had happened literally on the eve of it. When she got back to England she would be jobless, and she was feeling anxious in case she was going to be jobless for very long. Having been wantonly extravagant and refused to cancel this holiday, she couldn't afford to be without a practical means of support for many weeks.

Fernandez looked surprised, and then his black brows drew together in a frown. Being Spanish he also felt rather shocked, which was given away by his expression.

"But your parents?" he asked. "Have you no parents? Are you alone in the world?"

18

She admitted that she had been without parents since her last year at school, but there had been a little money left for her to train, and she had taken a course in child welfare. She had had two jobs as nursery-governess, one as governess to an older child, and the job that had just come to an end in such a unfortunate manner had combined so many duties that she had been more or less a maid-of-all-work. She wasn't ashamed of confessing this to the man across the table—perhaps because she was so sure she would never see him again after tonight, and in any case there was little point in departing from the truth—and she saw him looking at her in an inexplicable fashion, as if she was something he had never met before.

"Then although I said you don't look like Cinderella," he remarked, "your future is really as uncertain as Cinderella's."

"Yes." She stared down at the bubbles that were expanding and contracting in her wineglass. "Except that from the moment Cinderella lost her slipper things started to work out well for her!"

"That is true. It is a pity we cannot think of something that would enable things to work out well for you."

She looked across at him without speaking.

"Tell me," he requested, "what, exactly, are your qualifications — your accomplishments? You said that you have acted as governess to an older child. Presumably that was not as easy as looking after little ones? Were you a success when you undertook that particular task? Or was it, seeing that you are rather young yourself, just a little beyond you?" smiling to soften the inference in his words.

"No; I was quite a success. The child was at home from school for a year, owing to illness, and I think I helped her quite a lot. At any rate," with a reminiscent look of affection in her clear grey eyes, "we grew fond of one another, and it

19

was quite a wrench for both of us when school loomed up once more on the curriculum."

"You mean when you had to part?"

"Yes. And as a matter of fact we still correspond—not only I and the child, but the child's parents. They were very good to me."

He studied her reflectively.

"Possibly it would be easy to be good to you if you were doing what you English call 'pulling your weight'."

Once again she was silent, but her heart seemed to be bounding more quickly than normal —which no doubt was the effect of the wine, which was rather heady.

"Let me tell you something, Miss Waring," he said suddenly. "I am a doctor—what you call a 'consultant' doctor—in Madrid, and my home is, of course, in Madrid also. I have a motherless daughter of nine who was critically ill for several months, and now that she is on the mend I have explained that I wish her to live for a time on the coast. Here on the Costa Brava. I think I have found a suitable villa, or cottage, and Gianetta will be in the charge of her English nurse. But the nurse is not quite up to coping with Gia — perhaps for the reason that Gia is something of a monkey," smiling with a magical softening of his dark eyes, "and it seems to me that what is really needed is a governess. Someone young, and alive, and understanding—perhaps like yourself!"

"You mean——?"

Lisa felt her heart stop beating, and then rush on again wildly.

"I mean that it might solve your problem, and mine, if you stayed on here in San Cecilio, and accepted a position with a Spanish family. That is to say, if you would allow *me* to become your employer."

20

Lisa was quite certain that it was the wine that had got up into her head — that she ought to have stuck to only one glass, instead of accepting another half glass as well, and that being extremely potent it was already having a disastrous effect! She was imagining that she heard things — imagining that *he*, of all men, was offering her a job!

He regarded her quizzically as she appeared to be trying to take in his suggestion — groping for words to answer him.

"Perhaps you do not feel that you could take very easily to the Spanish way of life?" he suggested. "It is pleasant for a holiday, but how would it work out if you had to remain here in this country for a period of several months — at any rate until the autumn? Is that what you are asking yourself?"

She shook her head, and he thought that the dazed look in her eyes — so large and steady and English — was a trifle excessive.

"No. I would love to stay, but . . . you know nothing about me, she reminded him. How could you offer me a position with your own daughter when you know nothing about me?"

"True," he agreed, in a common-sense tone that was like a douche of clear cold water on her eager wonder. All at once everything was reduced to its proper perspective, and if her ego had been a bubble that could be pricked it could not have collapsed or become shrivelled more quickly. "But I can find out. You can supply me with the address of the parents of the child who was ill, and I can get in touch with them—also, perhaps, your most recent employer. But do not be afraid that I shall be influenced very much by anything she says, although I do feel it will be as well if I do make contact with her. For the sake of my daughter's welfare, you understand?" he ended in grave, quiet tones.

"Of course."

But there was just one moment when she wondered whether she did want to remain in Spain. He was charming and kind and courteous, this man — this doctor from Madrid — but beneath his kindness there was a thread of something inflexible, something that made her think of steel, and just about as unbending.

He could be adamant, if he chose, and his charm was the unfailing charm of his race. It resulted from his Latin blood, and put that suggestion of warm fires into eyes that could no doubt also look as bleak as ice.

He sensed that she was hesitating.

"Well," he said softly, "it is up to you. If you wish to stay, and my inquiries are satisfactory, then there is a position that I can offer you, here in San Cecilio. And in the meantime you can remain at your hotel a few days longer at my expense. Is that as you would wish it, *señorita*?

"I can afford to stay on a few days longer myself," she told him.

He rose politely, as if an interview was ended.

"Nevertheless, I think it will be at my expense."

When he left her in the entrance to the hotel she was hardly aware how she said goodnight to him. She went up in the lift to her room, and then out on to her balcony, where she looked upwards at the stars blazing like diamonds scattered broadcast across a pall of velvet tight-stretched above San Cecilio.

The stars of San Cecilio! . . . She would remember them always, whatever happened to her, wherever she went!

CHAPTER THREE

BUT IT seemed that for a time, at least, San Cecilio was to claim her.

Three days later she found herself having lunch in the Hotel Carabela with Dr. Fernandez and his daughter Gia. Gia was plainer than ever at close quarters, and this caused Lisa to wonder what her partly English mother must have been like, since there was no doubt about it, Dr. Fernandez was extraordinarily handsome. The only striking feature possessed by her father that the child had inherited was his thick black eyelashes, and between them her greenish-hazel eyes twinkled constantly. They were alert to everything that was going on around her, and although otherwise she was puny the eyes indicated a mental health and vigor that would be difficult to quench.

"You don't speak English like Miss Grinthorpe," she said, studying Lisa with interest across the lunch table. "She doesn't like me to call her Nannie, because she says that makes her feel old, so I call her Grimmie. Will you expect me to call you Miss Waring?"

"You can call me what you like," Lisa responded, smiling at her in the way she reserved for young people.

It was a smile that seldom failed.

"You don't *look* like Grimmie," Gia told her, crinkling up her eyes as she went on studying her. "You're pretty — isn't she, Papa?" appealing to her father.

He looked down dryly at the grapefruit she was engaged in spooning rather carelessly up to her mouth.

"It is extremely rude to make comments on anyone's appearance while they can overhear those comments," he reminded her, and then added: "Ah, I was afraid that would happen!" as a segment of grapefruit landed in her candy-pink-striped cotton lap, and she instantly looked extra-ordinarily guilty. "However Grimmie behaves, and however she looks, she doesn't seem to have improved your table manners!"

"I'm sorry, Papa," she whispered, and to Lisa she sounded abject. *"Lo siento mucho,"* she added in Spanish.

But his austere face did not relax, and for a few moments Lisa was not merely surprised, but indignant on Gianetta's behalf. She was so openly anxious to do everything she could to please her father, but on the whole she met with a surprising lack of appreciation, and very little encourage-ment. Perhaps it was his nature to be critical with young people, even a motherless only daughter.

"It's nothing very much to worry about," she remarked, as she leaned forward to deal with the stain on the cotton frock with her own table napkin. "There! There's hardly a mark!" after rubbing very hard for a second or so. "And, in any case," smiling into the small, downcast face, "worse things happen at sea!"

"Do they?" Gia inquired gravely.

"Much worse." With a few neat movements with her fingers Lisa had Gia's napkin securely tucked into the front of her dress, so that for the remainder of the meal it would be safe. "That's an English saying—a colloquialism. I expect you have lots of them in Spanish."

Rising like a small fish to the bait, Gia tried to remember as many proverbs and quotations as she could, and while her nimble mind was thus employed her temporary gloom left her, and although her father did not join in the light-hearted conversation that followed this did not seem to worry her. He sat watching them and smoking a cigarette until the coffee arrived, and then he said quietly to Lisa:

"I am having another look at the cottage I have all but decided to rent this afternoon, so would you care to come along and have a look at it, too?"

"Oh, yes," Lisa answered at once. And then she added a trifle more diffidently: "At least, I'd like to if — if you think it is likely to become in any way my concern? I mean, if you are still thinking seriously of employing me?"

"I have received a reply to my telegraphed request for information concerning you," he told her, in a level tone, "and it is quite satisfactory. It only remains for you to be convinced that I am a suitable employer, and we must think up some way of providing you with this satisfaction. I can put you in touch with my solicitor, or something of the sort, in Madrid——"

"Oh, but that isn't necessary," she assured him softly.

His eyebrows ascended in the way that made her feel young and inexperienced, and also perhaps a trifle *gauche*.

"It is as important for you to have no doubt about me as a man who will pay your salary, and be in a sense responsible for you and your well-being so long as you remain in Spain, as it is for me to feel certain that my child will be safe in your keeping," he pointed out, and for no rhyme or reason she colored. *Be in a sense responsible for you!* . . . It sounded so odd when she had watched him night after night for a fortnight and more, and never expected even to get to know him! "You see that?" he asked.

"Oh, yes—yes," she assured him earnestly, "I do see it!"

"That is as well," he returned dryly. "In your unprotected position you cannot afford to neglect any precaution that safeguards your welfare."

And she wondered whether he was rebuking her for her casual English method of picking up acquaintances.

His car was huge and white, with maroon upholstery, and in it they were soon driving at considerable speed along the coast. Gia sat on the back seat, where her father had ordered her to dispose of herself, and Lisa sat beside him at the wheel. A tentative suggestion that there was plenty of room for Gia to share the front seat with them, or that she should sit on Lisa's own lap, had met with an instant rebuff.

"I want to talk to you," he told her. "And little pitchers — to quote another of your English proverbs — have long ears," with that note of dryness in his voice she was getting to know so well.

But although he had said he wanted to talk to her they did not talk on the outward drive to the villa. Occasionally he pointed out to her a feature of interest; a lighthouse on a promontory jutting out into the peacock-blue sea, some rocks that had received a name which suited them, and about which stories were told, a torrent of brilliant growth that trespassed on to the highway. He told her the names of the flowers, and likened them to a less flamboyant specimen to be found in England, and when asked whether he knew England admitted that he did.

"Well?" Lisa couldn't refrain from asking.

"Quite well," he assented, but his reply suggested that he did not wish to pursue the subject.

For the most part she lay back against the luxuriously well-sprung seat and watched his slim, tanned hands on the wheel, realizing that although the high-powered car was being more or less put on its mettle he was driving superbly on a road that grew steadily steeper and more difficult to negotiate. The afternoon was full of heat and languor around them; the Pyrenees

26

inland were dark as a violet sky save where the winter snows lingered on the peaks like caps of sugar icing, and fields of lavender and linseed were bright against that sombre wall. And always on one side of them was the sea, sparkling with every tone of blue from turquoise to the most vivid kingfisher, and the white beach fell farther and farther away below them until the people on it were mere specks, and so were the orange and scarlet sun-umbrellas.

They sped through sleepy villages and past white huddled cottages, and encountered little traffic at that hour of siesta. The aromatic scent of pines floated in the air, and pines seemed to crown every knoll and rise.

When at last they drew up outside the villa it was after penetrating a thicket of pines, and they seemed to rise in a guardian wall around them as they sat in the sudden silence which followed the switching off of the car engine.

Gia, on the back seat, was too used to white-walled buildings and green-tiled roofs and tassels of flaming blossoms that dripped like flame against the windows to be excited by what she saw, but Lisa felt as if the breath actually caught in her throat with pleasure and admiration. There were green-painted curly wrought-iron grilles to the balconies, a damask rose twined itself about one of them, and the front door was solid dark oak like the door of a church, and banded with iron also like the door of a church.

Inside there was a black and white tiled hall, and a baroque staircase curving up to the bedrooms. The staircase also overflowed into a kind of gallery, and the walls were hung with portraits, which seemed very impressive for a holiday villa. The furnishings were not precisely holiday furnishings, either, for they had been chosen with care, and were mostly period pieces, while the rugs and the silken curtains, the cushions and the ornaments made Lisa wonder what would happen if they were damaged in any way. She had no knowledge — no real knowledge, that is — of works of art, but she thought she recognized a Tintoretto in the library, and there was an exquisite Greek bronze on a pedestal that aroused all her admiration.

Dr. Fernandez watched her looking about her in a slightly awed fashion, and explained:

"This house belongs to a friend of mine, and actually I have already agreed to take it for a period of at least a year. It will be left exactly as it is, and there is a housekeeper to look after the place, and her husband attends to the outside. At the moment they are on holiday, but they can be recalled almost imediately. Could you move in here in a couple of days?"

Lisa looked a little surprised, and then answered:

"Yes, of course." She hesitated a moment, and then asked: "Will Miss Grimthorpe be coming here, too?"

"No, I have decided to pay her a month's wages and send her back to England. Her accent is not good, and Gia is too old, I think, for a nurse now. She must learn to look after herself more, and you will act the part of a governess-companion to her."

"I see," Lisa said.

Actually she was thinking—So that was how he did it! Just sent people about their business, when he no longer had any use for them, and paid them a month's salary to salve any hurt feelings!... Was that what would happen to her one day?

She felt that he was watching her rather closely, in the dimness of the hall.

"You think that you will be lonely? Just you and Gia?"

28

"Oh, no," she denied instantly. "And there will be the housekeeper and her husband."

"Precisely. And I shall come here myself sometimes — and perhaps bring friends."

"I see," she said again.

They passed out from the dimness into the vivid tangle of the garden, and Lisa thought that although it really was rather a wilderness — proof, perhaps, that the housekeeper's husband was old — it was the most beautiful wilderness she had ever seen. There were roses so huge and so darkly exotic that she seldom remembered seeing any like them before, and the high white walls were overhung by pale mauve growth like clematis, and starry jasmine flowers. There were green tunnels of cypress, almond and orange trees, crazy-paved walks, and a huge patio on to which the main rooms opened, and where the light would linger after the sun had gone down. There was also a way down to the beach, which Julio Fernandez pointed out to her, smiling in the way that suddenly lighted up his dark face when he suggested that she might teach Gianetta to swim.

"That is, of course, if you swim yourself," he said.

"Yes, I do," she answered.

He glanced at her for an instant, and perhaps in that instant he saw her denuded of her crisp linen dress and clothed only in a brief swim-suit, her almost childishly slender figure tanned to gold by the kiss of his Spanish sun. Then he looked away, and presently he wandered away by himself, and Gia and Lisa wandered alone in the Sleeping-Beauty wilderness.

Gia's eyes were not too certain as she gazed about her.

"Will it not seem strange," she suggested, "just the two of us in this big house, and my Papa not here?"

"But he will come sometimes," Lisa reminded her. "You heard him say so."

"Yes." But Gia sighed unexpectedly. "And he will bring friends. That means he will bring Doña de Camponelli!"

Lisa looked at her for explanation.

"And who is she?" she asked, while her heart missed a beat.

Gia looked up at her with her greenish-hazel eyes full of an unchildlike but very definite displeasure.

"Doña Beatriz de Camponelli—someone who Grimmie says will marry my papa! In Madrid she comes to see us often, and once here she came to see Papa. She is beautiful, like my mama, who was gathered to the Holy Angels when I was born. She and my mama were cousins, but I do not like her, although I would have liked very much to have known my mama!"

Something in the plaintive voice, and the sigh that followed the words, touched Lisa inexpressibly, and she reached out and drew the small figure close to her in an almost protective hug. Then she thought she saw the pieces of a jigsaw puzzle falling into place. . . . The ravishing, red-haired woman who had dined with Dr. Fernandez, the fact that he had so little noticeable fondness for his daughter—no doubt his heart had been broken when his wife died, and man-like he had blamed the child! — and now, after nearly nine years, he was going to console himself with the cousin who was so like his wife!

Perhaps his daughter's plainness, when his wife had been so beautiful, offended him, too, and that was one reason why he was sharp with her.

Unnecessarily sharp. . . .

But as they walked back to the car Lisa had the feeling that the villa was not such a delightful place after all, and that the overgrown garden was an offence rather than a place in which one would wish to linger. Even the sun seemed to fall less goldenly, and the pines had the effect of shutting one in.

If she came here to live she would never leave it as she came to it — its hallmark would fall across her heart, just as the shadow of the pines cut across the flagged floor of the patio, but, unlike that shadow, leaving an indelible imprint.

She was so sure of that that she climbed into the car in absolute silence, and Dr. Fernandez looked at her rather curiously as he started up the engine.

CHAPTER FOUR

ON THE WAY back he did ask her a few questions of a strictly personal nature, and she answered them automatically, as if she was still struggling to throw off the depressing effects of those last few moments at the villa.

"You must forgive me if I appear to be prying into your life," the doctor said, "but under the circumstances I would like everything to be as clear as possible. You have really no ties at all in your own country?"

"No." She appeared to hesitate for a moment. "No real ties, that is."

"What do you mean by that?"

"Well, I have only distant relatives." Her smile was fugitive, and struck him as a little wistful. "And they hardly count, do they?"

"Not in England, perhaps," he admitted. "But in Spain we are rather addicted to family gatherings, and in fact the family is very important to the heart of every Spaniard. We do not drift apart and lose touch as you people seem to do." He frowned at the road ahead as if the English and their methods were not altogether approved of by him, and she found herself wondering what sort of circle he moved in in Madrid, and whether that thin, clever face meant that he was at the zenith of his profession, as she strongly suspected that he was. For not only did he look clever, but the aura of exclusiveness and expensiveness that surrounded him were the usual accompaniments of success. "In Spain, for instance, a young woman of your age would hardly be wandering about looking for some means of suporting herself. Some member of her family would almost certainly have taken her under their wing, and she would probably be married, or arrangements for her marriage would have been carried through on her behalf."

"Instead of which in England we prefer to make our own arrangements for marriage—if, and when, we decide we would like to be married," she added crisply, while he continued to stare at the road ahead as if his main absorption was his driving.

He shrugged his shoulders slightly,

"I was merely pointing out to you that in this country your position would have been more secure. However," as he negotiated a sudden sharp bend in the road, "what I was trying to find out was just how free you are to do as you choose, and whether there were any ties apart from ties of blood that might make you feel homesick for England after you had been here a few weeks?"

"You mean"—she felt herself flushing brilliantly, although he was not looking at her— "you mean, I might be — I might be engaged?"

"You wear no betrothal ring, but your heart could be involved." The tiniest smile touched his lips as she glanced at him sideways.

"I—no, I'm not . . . I mean, there is no one!"

"That is as I would prefer it," he told her, as if a minor obstacle had been removed from his path. "You will settle down more easily if there are no emotional entanglemnts linking you with your own country, and no sudden feelings of nostalgia likely to come between you and your job. I'm afraid I demand efficiency and concentration in those I employ, and a single-minded attentiveness to my affairs." He sent her a look from his brilliant dark eyes. "Is that too much to ask of you, Miss Waring? Remember it is my only child I am entrusting to your care, and you will be left very much to your own devices while I am not here!"

"Yes. Yes, I realize that." But Lisa experienced another of those moments when she wondered whether after all she ought to allow herself to be employed by him — whether it wouldn't be wiser suddenly to change her mind, and make her apologies. There was something curiously cold-blooded about the way he referred to her *emotional entanglements,* as if he half expected her to give a guarantee of immunity from any such entanglement while, at least, she remained in his employ. "Perhaps," she suggested suddenly, "you would like to make more exhaustive enquiries about me before you seriously consider allowing me to take charge of your little girl?"

"No." He shook his head as if he saw nothing strange about the suggestion, but had already made up his mind. "I have a feeling that you and Gia will get on well together, and that is the important thing. Also, if we can get the housekeeper and her husband back tomorrow— and they are not very far away, so that should be quite simple — I would like you to move in to the villa the day after tomorrow, and Gina of course will move in with you."

"If you are *thoroughly* certain in your own mind that I shall give satisfaction?" she heard herself murmuring, wishing she was as thoroughly certain in her own mind that this Spanish interlude, which was to have been nothing more than an interlude, wasn't being unwisely prolonged.

When they got back to the hotel Miss Grim-thorpe appeared to take charge of Gianetta and Lisa thought she looked very sullen — not at all the type of constant companion she herself would have chosen for a child of nine. And the look she directed at Lisa was full of reproof, as if she considered that she had taken away her job, and a month's salary in lieu of notice was hardly a suitable recompense. Which should have spoken well for the job itself, Lisa realized, but her own

34

mind was too disturbed, and there were too many backthoughts to worry her, to permit such a thing as confidence to take any root just then.

She bathed and changed for dinner, and in the hotel dining-room she was regaled by the sight of an empty table in the alcove where Dr. Fernandez always sat. But the flowers on the table were velvety scarlet roses, and they looked as if they were confident they would not remain unappreciated throughout the evening.

And, just as she was leaving the dining-room, Lisa saw the doctor enter by the other portion of the swing dors, and he was accompanied by the woman with the coils of red-gold hair wound about her shapely head. Doña Beatriz de Camponelli! For somehow Lisa had no doubts at all that this *was* Doña Beatriz.

She wore a black dress that was almost as striking as the golden one she had worn on the other occasion when she dined at the hotel, and about her shoulders was a gauzy stole that was iridescent with sequins. There were some blood-red stones at her throat, and instantly Lisa decided that the scarlet roses had been chosen to match them.

Lisa escaped as quickly as she could, before either of them saw her — or so she hoped — and outside on the terrace she was surprised when a page-boy handed her a note.

The note said simply, but with an authority that was barely overlaid by the straightforwardness of the phraseology:

"I shall be dining with a friend, but I would be glad if you join us for coffee on the terrace afterwards. I particularly wish my friend to meet you. J.F.."

J.F. — Julio Fernandez! Her new employer!

Lisa went down into the garden to wait until the moment when she might reasonably expect the others to appear upon the terrace, and from a point of vantage she saw them emerge from the dining-room The terrace was wide and decorated with huge urns cascading flowers and electric light bulbs, and from the windows behind it an additional flood of light streamed. Dr. Fernandez and his guest made their way to one of the discreetly arranged tables, and Lisa noticed immediately that it was a table for three.

She ascended the terrace steps with a feeling of diffidence, and while a waiter hurried forward to receive the doctor's order stood silhouetted against the velvety night. She was wearing a flowered chiffon dress, very unostentatious, very much inclined to emphasize the extreme slenderness of her build, so that she looked like a gossamer-draped wraith with the star-pricked gloom behind her, and only her lovely cap of hair shone with a living lustre. Sometimes she tied it back with a ribbon, but tonight it was falling softly to her shoulders, and the rays of light reached out and drew attention to its corn-silk beauty.

Dr. Fernandez stood up, and accorded her a slight smile. His companion remained seated, but looked up with distinct curiosity.

"May I introduce Doña de Camponelli," Fernandez said, after he had presented Lisa to the exquisite redhead. "And what," he asked, as she sank into a chair, "will you drink with your coffee? A liqueur?"

"No, thank you. Just coffee," Lisa answered, and folded her hands a little primly on her lap. This was so unlike the night they had shared a bottle of wine on the waterfront that she could feel the formality stiffening her limbs, and Doña de Camponelli was watching her with a gleam of amusement in her eyes.

"You must forgive me for saying so," she said, "but you are quite unlike any children's governess I have met before. They usually conform to a sort of pattern, and have an air of repressed authority

36

about them. But you look rather as if you have only just emerged from the schoolroom yourself!"

Lisa could not help feeling herself belittled by this observation.

"I am not quite as young as I look," she remarked.

"Then that is perhaps as well, if you are to have any control over an imp like Gianetta." Her sloe-black, slumbrous eyes, with the cool amusement still glinting in them, swung round languidly to the doctor. "Are you *quite* sure you aren't making a mistake, *querido*? I had no liking for your dour Miss Grimthorpe, but at least she had years on her side, and years bestow experience! Miss Waring can have had so little experience that it is like thrusting an unfair burden on her shoulders to expect her to take entire charge of Gia."

"I don't think so." The doctor was grinding a cigarette out in an ash-tray at his elbow, and then she offered his case to Lisa. The Spanish woman, she was to discover, did not smoke, and apart from a highly provocative shade of lipstick she used little or no make-up. But her complexion was so flawless, her features so perfect, that she did not need it. "Miss Waring may look young, but she has already confessed to me that she is twenty-four, and that is far removed from the schoolroom," with a smile at Lisa that warmed her heart for a moment, although his dinner guest's next words dissipated the warmth.

"In this country twenty-four might mean something, but in England young women develop slowly. Have you had previous employers, Miss Waring?" she asked, and Lisa was conscious of a distinct sensation of shock as the realization struck home that in spite of the look of humor that was stamped upon her face Doña Beatriz de Camponelli was hostile to her — hostile from the very outset.

"I, er — why, yes," Lisa answered awkwardly. "Dr. Fernandez has already taken up my references."

"In so short a time?" with a quizzical quirk to the painted mouth.

Julio Fernandez looked surprised.

"There has been plenty of time," he remarked. "And the references were entirely satisfactory."

Doña Beatriz laid a hand — an exquisite hand that blazed with rings — upon his arm.

"Forgive me, *mi querido*," she said softly, "if I seem to doubt your judgment, but there is such a thing as being over-hasty sometimes. And from what you have told me you and Miss Waring do not really know very much of one another. An acquaintance struck up while she is on holiday! The situation is unorthodox, to say the least!" She smiled in a strange, cold, arch fashion across at the English girl. "And from your point of view, Miss Waring, it could be disastrous — accepting a position in a household unknown to you. And in a country completely unknown to you. But on that head, at least, I can reassure you — you could not be more fortunate than to be offered a position by Dr. Ferandez, particularly when it involves the care of his only daughter."

Lisa was silent. Dr. Fernandez, she thought, looked embarrassed.

"The good fortune is going to be mutual, I am quite certain," she heard him say. "And if you saw them together you would have no doubt that Miss Waring is absolutely right for Gia. The child took to her at once, and I predict that they are going to get along famously together. What do you say, Miss Waring?"

"I hope so," Lisa answered stiffly. "At least I shall do my best to improve upon the Nurse Grimthorpe interlude. A nurse is not good for a girl of nine. She would be better off at school."

"That is for Dr. Fernandez to say!" Doña Beatriz snapped, and then she looked at her diamond-studded wrist-watch. "I must be off, Julio! I am leaving for the airport at ten, and it is very nearly half-past nine." She gave him a languishing, regretful look—so regretful that Lisa felt acutely uncomfortable. "But we will meet again in Madrid in a few days? You will be leaving here the day after tomorrow?"

"Yes, after I have seen Miss Waring and Gia settled in at the villa."

The arrogant Spanish beauty held out her hand to Lisa — or, rather, she extended her gloved fingertips towards her.

"Take good care of Gia, Miss Waring," she said, as if she was laying an injunction upon her. "I have no doubt at all that we shall meet again before very long. I have Dr. Fernandez' interests very much at heart, and if he cannot visit you at the villa I shall certainly do so."

"We will both visit her at the villa," Dr. Fernandez promised.

When they had vanished into the darkness, presumably to enter a waiting car, Lisa got up and wandered away to the far end of the terrace, and from there she descended into the purple gloom of the garden. She felt distured and anxious, and almost upset. Never in her life had she come up against such naked hostility as that which Dona Beatriz had displayed towards her, and she felt that she wanted to wait for the doctor's return and then rush upon him and ask to be released from the obligation of working for him.

And then the thought of Gia, and the small hand that had stolen into hers that afternoon, affected her like a douche of common sense. The child was lonely, and needed her, and she herself needed someone to be responsible for. They could be happy together in that vivid garden by the sea, and she would be mad to turn down a first-class job — a job that Doña Beatriz had vouched for herself! — because a pair of slumbrous dark eyes with malicious dislike in them had gazed at her across a table on the terrace.

After all, so far as she knew Doña Beatriz *was* only a friend of Julio Fernandez — and she might never become anything more than a friend. It took two to come to a decision about such a thing as marriage, and the doctor had been a widower for nine years. Why had he waited all that time if the woman who was his wife's cousin had been ready and willing to become his wife (as, judging by her possessive attitude, she was), at more or less the drop of a handkerchief? Why hadn't she long ago become Señora Fernandez, and undertaken the selection of a governess for Gia herself?

Lisa spent a long time on the balcony outside her bedroom later that night trying to fathom this out. She did not know that two floors below her, almost exactly beneath her balcony, but with a good deal more space at his disposal, and a far more luxurious room behind him, Dr. Fernandez was doing the same thing.

He had returned to the hotel after driving his dinner-guest back to hers, and gone straight to his room, and started to smoke numerous thin Spanish cigarettes as he started to pace up and down. He didn't look exactly troubled, but there was a lack of ease in his expression as the light that was burning on his bedside table sent golden beams out to discover burnished lights in his sleek black hair, and enrich the pale olive of his complexion.

Tonight he was wearing a white flower in his buttonhole, and it was Beatriz's fingers that had plucked it on their way down the drive, and inserted it in the lapel of his dinner-jacket. He took it out and looked at it, and then absent-mindedly his long fingers played with it until it fell apart, and the petals went falling like snow over the balcony rail. He could hear Beatriz's voice saying softly, when she tucked the flower into his buttonhole:

"That is something that you can keep and remember me by until we meet again, Julio!" Her voice was honey-sweet and a trifle husky, and her eyes were heavy and languid as she lifted them to his face. But there was fire behind the languor, and he knew it, and because it was fire that sought to compel him he deliberately looked away, and reminded her that she had little time to lose if she was to leave her hotel at ten.

But in a couple of nights from now he would be back in Madrid, and Beatriz would be having dinner with him in his flat. It was a sumptuous flat, and because he had an excellent man-servant they often dined there together in preference to seeking a restaurant. Beatriz, being a widow, had no qualms about sharing the isolation of a man's flat, or any fears that her reputation would suffer if she did so, for everyone — or practically every single one of their mutual friends — expected they would marry one day, and she knew how to behave correctly. With Julio it would have been dangerous to do anything else!

He was not the susceptible type, not affected by such a thing as an altered glance, a new note introduced into an already lowered voice — at any rate, not noticeably. So Doña Beatriz had learned to be careful in her dealings with him, and in spite of the fact that he sometimes filled her with impatience, their friendship had an excessively immaculate quality about it, and she did not know that only lately he had begun to realize that it could not go on like that.

It was not fair to keep a woman as beautiful, of such unblemished reputation, and with so many friends as Doña Beatriz possessed, dangling on a thread, because he could not make up his mind about her.

For one thing there was the past, with its unhappiness and its bitterness, rising up around him so constantly even at this late stage, and Beatriz, even more than anyone else, knew all about that unhappiness. It would be like keeping it with him, chaining it to him always, to share it with her. And then there was the question of Gia — Gia disliked her. And as for himself . . .

He leaned over the balcony rail and stared upwards at the stars. He found his thoughts drifting. Somewhere in the hotel there was a young woman who looked as if she ought to have someone to take care of her, instead of accepting the responsibility for looking after someone else. She had hair that swung in a silken cloud to her shoulders, and there was a suggestion of moonbeams tangled up with cobwebs about it when the light streamed over it. Tonight she had looked very young and defenceless, in that gauzy, patterned dress of hers, and he had been able to tell immediately that Beatriz hadn't taken to her, Indeed, on that short journey down the drive to the spot where he had left his white-colored car she had stated quite definitely:

"I think you are making a mistake, Julio. That girl is not at all the right type for Gia. And in any case, if she were practical and reliable would she have spent all her money on such a thing as a holiday in a place like San Cecilio when she hadn't a job to go back to? She sounds to me much more like an adventuress! Did you really get in touch with her former employers and make inquiries about her?"

"No," Julio had answered, and she had looked really shocked.

"But, Julio! . . . *Chiquito,* are you mad?" she had demanded.

"Perhaps," and he had shrugged his shoulders slightly, dismissingly, as if he wished she wouldn't dwell upon the affair. "But I had the feeling she might be good for Gia."

"You had the feeling! . . ."

Doña Beatriz's eyes had suddenly sent forth sparks.

And now as he leaned on his balcony rail the man knew she was right. He had behaved quixotically, and he couldn't think why. The girl probably was an adventuress, and she had come to San Cecilio to look for a husband, or something of the sort. She looked young and unawakened, and he was fairly sure she was unawakened, but one could never tell. The best thing he could do would be to give her a month's trial, and then, if she wasn't satisfactory, pack her off home again.

If she wasn't satisfactory he would be quite ruthless about getting rid of her.

And then he returned to the problem of Madrid in a couple of nights' time. How did one continue to stave off the inevitable, when it was the inevitable?

CHAPTER FIVE

LISA AND GINETTA ran happily through all the
rooms at the villa, finding out all there was to find
out about them. The bedroms were luxurious,
and there were no fewer than six of them, and
of these the main three bedroms had private bath-
rooms attached. The rooms allocated to the
governess and her charge formed a kind of
nursery suite, and in the daytime they were very
bright and pleasant, and it was only at night
that Lisa found them a little lonely and cut off.

Of course, she could have dined downstairs in
state in the main dining-room, but Señora Cortina,
the housekeeper, might have thought it odd —
perhaps even inconsiderate — to be expected to
lay a huge dining-table for one, especially when
the room itself was so huge. So Lisa had a tray
upstairs in the suite with Gia, and on the whole
this was much more fun, because Señora Cortina
thought up amusing dishes for their evening meal,
and Gia had it in a dressing-gown after her bath,
and the atmosphere was very relaxed.

Señora Cortina was quite a character. She was
a shrivelled little Catalan woman, with a sharp
tongue and a very bright eye — especially when
her husband, who was her second husband, did
something to offend her. His job was to keep
the tangled wilderness of a garden in some sort
of order, but he was much older than she was,
and work seemed an effort to him. He much
preferred to sit with a pipe in the shade, while
the delectable smell of her spiced buns reached him
through the open doorway to the kitchen. Sometimes she relented after scolding him in a manner
that raised the echoes in the villa, and permitted
him to sample the buns. But sometimes the scold-
ings went on and on, and upstairs on her balcony,

with the evening calm around her, Lisa wondered where such a diminutive woman got so much energy from.

But she recognized in the housekeeper a completely trustworthy type, with her employer's interests at heart, and with no outside assistance she kept the interior of the villa at a shining pitch of perfection. Every piece of mellowed oak shone, silver fairly dazzled the eye, and the household linens and other fabrics were looked after religiously. And in addition to all this Señora Cortina was really a splendid cook. Lisa had never sampled fish soup until she arrived in Spain, but Señora Cortina's fish soup left an echo in the mind, like a piece of pleasing harmony. She could do things with chopped nuts, honey and raisins and ice-cream that left an even more indelible impression, and Lisa knew she would never forget her new-baked bread. Such bread had nothing to do with bakers' shops. It was something to start the day on in a contented frame of mind.

She and Gina had their day fairly well planned once they had been at the villa a week. In the mornings they did lessons in English, and Gia helped Lisa improve her Spanish. This had the effect of causing Gia to concentrate on the grammar of her own language, and was therefore of benefit to herself as well as the governess.

The afternoons were too hot for anything apart from siesta — at any rate, the early part of the afternoon. And after tea they went down on to the beach.

Sometimes in the early mornings, too, they visited the beach. And it was on one of their morning excursions to the glorious strip of shelving sand, at the edge of which the larkspur seas encroached, that Lisa ran literally into the arms of a young man she had known for one brief week-end as Peter Hamilton-Tracey.

Before Señora Cortina took her hot breakfast rolls out of the oven, and the smell of freshly-made coffee filled every corner of her kitchen, the atmosphere in the villa garden was as cool and sparkling as an English summer morning. The roses sparkled with dew, and it hung in great diamond drops on the glossy green leaves of the orange-trees. The scent of the pines was moist and earthy and penetrating.

Down on the beach the sea came rolling in without any of that oily swell that made it seem leaden during the heat of the day, and the green and gold uncovered rocks looked like green and gold monsters against the incredible purity of the sky, with the rosy flush of sunrise dying out of it. Wearing cotton sun-suits, and with their hair streaming out behind them, Lisa and Gia had formed the habit of racing out to and clambering over these rocks, and sometimes they sat for a quarter of an hour or so while the sun climbed higher in the sky, and the bleached beach became a stretch of burning gold, acquiring a tan which in both cases was badly needed.

Gia looked painfully thin in a swim-suit, but her sunsuits were beautifully cut and expensive, like everything else in her wardrobe. When unpacking for her, Lisa had wondered who selected these delicious outfits for her, and once again it had struck her that Dr. Fernandez must be rather more than a man of substance.

By contrast even with Gia's gay little bathing-costume, Lisa's was neat and unpretentious. But already her skin was turning to gold, and her hair gleamed like molten gold in the sunshine. When she was playing on the edge of the water — not being nearly a strong enough swimmer to risk giving Gia any instruction, particularly as she had absolutely no knowledge of the currents that affected that part of the coast—Gia stood on the rocks and called to her that she looked like a mermaid, and afterwards they would race back across the sands to the villa.

She was running at full tilt, with a delighted Gia attempting to catch her, when a man on his way to bathe suddenly strolled round a rock, and, appearing in her path too suddenly for her to avoid him, opened his arms to catch her.

Gasping, she clung to him for a moment, and he smiled white-toothed at her.

"Well, well!" he exclaimed. "Well, well!"

The fact that he spoke in English was an immediate relief, and then she knew as she poured forth apologies that she was looking up into a face that was familiar. Not a face she had got to know very well, but she had seen it before.

It was bronzed and typically English, the eyes blue and audacious, the hair a glowing thatch as yellow as her own.

"Why," Lisa exclaimed, as if she could hardly believe the evidence of her own eyes, "you are — you must be! — you're Mr. Hamilton-Tracey's brother!"

"Peter," he supplied. "Peter Hamilton-Tracey. But," looking down at her with frowning brows, although his eyes still laughed, "I don't think I remember you. Am I supposed to know you?"

She carefully extricated herself from the lightness of his hold, and stepped back a pace or two on the sand. She shook her head, so that her hair swung like a cape.

"No, I don't think so. At least" — there was the glimmer of a smile in her own eyes as she looked up at him—"you saw me once, but it's hardly likely you would remember me. At that time I wore a uniform — a linen dress with a white collar and cuffs — and my hair was short. I've allowed it to grow in the last six months."

"Have you?" He looked at it apreciatively. "And a very wise thing to do, too, if I may be permitted to say so! But . . . a *linen* dress, with *a white collar and cuffs*! . . ." He whistled suddenly. "Were you in charge of infants? My brother's infants?"

"I was." She looked down demurely at her present charge, and Gia slipped a hand into hers and held it tight as if she didn't altogether enjoy this sudden encounter.

"Then of course I remember you!" But Lisa was certain he was merely trying to make up for a lack of gallantry. "And you must have had the patience of Job to put up with those two children of John's! I'm their uncle, but talk about a couple of pestilential imps! . . ." And then he seemed to become aware that Gia was looking at him very doubtfully indeed, and he tweaked an end of her lank hair. "Hullo!" he said. "Are you the present incumbent?"

Gia's English wasn't apparently quite up to that one, and Lisa translated for her.

"This gentleman means am I looking after you, am I am, aren't I? And that means that I must take you back to breakfast before Señora Cortina wonders what has become of us, and starts getting in touch with the police." She nodded in a friendly fashion at Peter Hamilton-Tracey. "Good-bye, Mr. Hamilton-Tracey," she said, rather shyly. "It's strange that we should have met again so far from our own country."

But the man wasn't going to let her go after such a brief interchange—not that she looked like a sea-nymph with that golden tangle of hair caressing her bare shoulders, her blue and white sun-suit crisp in the sunshine. her slim legs like a schoolgirl's terminating in pretty, shapely feet with natural pink toe-nails. She was much too good to let go altogether, without any hope of seeing her again, and he simply couldn't understand how he could ever possibly have forgotten her, having seen her once.

"You must let me know where you're staying, and where I can get in touch with you," he begged. "After all, we're both English, and . . ." He looked into her smoke-grey eyes, and thought that they were certainly very English. "Please! I can't even remember your name," he confessed wryly.

She told him.

"Elizabeth Waring."

"How unlike the Costa Brava that sounds," he commented.

And then he admitted that he had been ill, and that an artist friend had placed at his disposal a tiny cottage, where he looked after himself, and was beginning to feel much more like himself again.

"You mean that you have no one at all to look after you?" she asked.

"Oh, there's a woman who comes in to do the cleaning, and she does a certain amount of shopping for me, but I cook and do all the rest myself." He smiled at her. "You must come and have tea with me one day."

"I'm afraid the local inhabitants would not approve of that."

"Well, perhaps not," he agreed, grinning a little. "You'd have to bring a duenna with you, wouldn't you? Then will you let me come and call upon you, wherever you're staying?"

In the end they agreed to meet on the beach the following morning, and the meeting was repeated the following morning, and the morning after that. Lisa saw nothing wrong in just foregathering with a fellow-countryman on the beach, particularly as they were in full view of anyone who cared to study them. and although Gia was bashful at first, and declined to have very much to do with the Englishman, after the second morning she unbent, and by the fourth and fifth they were on excellent terms.

Lisa, who had been nervous of permitting Gia to enter the water while she was alone with her, had every confidence in entrusting her to the care of Peter, who seemed to take a liking to the small, plain Spanish child, with the enormous green eyes that made him think there was something elf-like about her. And after a few nervous essays on the edge of the water she gradually gained enough confidence to allow him to teach her a simple breast-stroke, which was followed by a sudden rush of enthusiasm to emulate everything he did.

But while permitting her to believe she was making enormous strides he was very careful of her, and it was sheer ill fortune that a threatening bilous attack brought about an onset of queasiness when she entered the water on the sixth morning after Peter Hamilton-Tracey had suddenly appeared on their limited horizon.

Only the night before Lisa had been thinking it strange that she had heard nothing from Madrid, and that after telephoning to make certain they were quite all right on the first night after their arrival Dr. Fernandez had suddenly seemed to assume that all must be well. He had written once, and sent Lisa a cheque for a generous month's salary in advance, but that was all she had heard from him. And there had been no message for Gia in the letter.

But now, all at once, while Gia started to tread water wildly and rush back to the beach as if she was either in pain or sudden fright — and she was afflicted by both the physical and the mental disturbance — a car drew up on the coast road, and two people alighted and came across the sands to them.

Lisa took one look at the car and recognized it at once. She would know those long white lines anywhere. And the man in the light lounge suit, with a carelessly flowing tie and hair like black silk in the sunshine — he was known to her even better than the car. And the woman who accompanied him could be none other than Doña Beatriz de Camponelli.

Doña Beatriz obviously didn't believe in beach wear, or even informal holiday wear. Her silk suit was as impeccable as if she was going out to lunch at one of Madrid's most exclusive clubs or restaurants, and the perilous high heels of her shoes were a menace to her ankles as she walked awkwardly across the yielding sand. The only concession to informality was the fact that she carried her large white cartwheel hat in her hand, so that her lovely red head was exposed to the caresses of the salt sea air and the sun.

Gia hurled herself into Lisa's arms, burst into a flood of stormy weeping, and then when she caught sight of her father absolutely rushed at him. He picked her up and, in spite of the detriment to his immaculate suit, carried her quite gently back to Lisa, and then knelt in the sand beside her to examine her. She celebrated his arrival by being violently sick, and crying out that she had swallowed a lot of sea-water.

Doña Beatriz turned shocked and coldly disapproving eyes from Lisa to the tall, fair, handsome young man, wearing the briefest bathing-trunks, who had by this time joined the group.

"Can it be," Doña Beatriz inquired, in her musical English, "that you are a friend of Miss Waring here?"

"Why, yes," he answered instantly, looking faintly surprised, but he was also concerned because Gia was undoubtedly far from well — though it was not due to any sea-water she had swallowed. At least he was prepared to vouch for that.

But while the Spanish woman looked vaguely triumphant, Dr. Fernandez looked up from his daughter.

"We will get her back to the house," he said quietly, and he had hardly glanced at Lisa. "She is obviously suffering from some upset. It could be a touch of sun, or something she has eaten."

"Or sea-water she has swallowed," Dona Beatriz said distinctly. "Perhaps Miss Waring was too busy with her friend to notice that Gia was in difficulties, and if the child has been taught to swim almost certainly she *was* in difficulties! Children of that age don't lie!"

CHAPTER SIX

THEY RETURNED to the villa, and for the remainder
of that day Lisa knew that she wasn't merely
under a cloud, she was highly suspect, and strongly
disapproved of.

Doña Beatriz didn't attempt to conceal that
she considered that Lisa had been put upon trial,
and had ingloriously failed to justify any further
belief in her, and that the sensible thing would
be to replace her immediately. It didn't matter
that, once having been put to bed and treated by
her father for an ordinary upset stomach, Gia
recovered rapidly, and admitted that she had
never at any time been in difficulties in the
water, and on the contrary had been thoroughly
enjoying herself until something inside her turned
queasy. It didn't matter that, just before he somewhat awkwardly dissociated himself from the
group, and walked off towards his own cottage,
Peter Hamilton-Tracey attempted to put in a
good word for Lisa, and assured Dr. Fernandez
that there had been no neglect whatsoever on
her part, and that she was completely wonderful
with children, as he had reason to know since she
had looked after his brother's — although since
he hadn't remembered her when they met again
Lisa herself would have doubted this recommenda-
tion! — and looked concerned at what had
occurred.

Nothing, apparently, mattered apart from the
fact that a father had been caused justifiable
vexation, if nothing worse, and Doña Beatriz was
in a position to offer advice, which she obviously
did very freely.

Once she had discarded her wet swim-suit, and
donned a more suitable cotton frock, Lisa had
hurried to her charge's room, and assisted her

employer in everything that he did for his daughter She had received curt instructions not to leave the child for an instant while he fetched a case (without which, apparently, he never travelled from his car), and dosed the invalid; and when, feeling slightly more like herself, Gia managed a wan smile, and attempted to snuggle for comfort into Lisa's arms, an even curter instruction to allow her to lie flat was issued immediately. Gia looked as if she might dissolve into tears, Lisa colored, and the child protested:

"But I *want* Lisa to hold my hand! And I like to feel her close. And I'm better now."

"You will be better if you behave yourslf, and do exactly as I tell you you must do," the doctor returned, so shortly that, for an instant, Lisa experienced a flaring of anger against him because he could adopt such a tone to a small sufferer. But he gave her no opportunity to say anything herself, for he went on: "It is wiser that she should be quite undisturbed for a time now, and not fussed over in any way. And if I can trust you to sit with her——"

Lisa's color burned in her cheeks as if it would burn holes in them.

"I *think* you can trust me to do that," she replied quietly. "And I shall do nothing to upset her."

He sent her an odd, considering look.

"Well, it wasn't a particularly severe upset, so she should be all right in a few hours. And I shall be here now!"

The way he said, "And I shall be here now!" suggested that he was interposing a rampart between his only child and someone who might carelessly — perhaps with reprehensible carelessness! — do her harm.

When he had left the room Lisa sat expecting a visitation from Doña Beatriz, but the hours wore away and the lovely Spanish woman did not once come to make inquiries in the sick-room. Perhaps, Lisa decided, she had no great liking for sick-rooms, as such; and having arrived, and created a certain amount of consternation as a result of her arrival, she was satisfied with the results so far. For naturally the English girl would be feeling less sure of her job, and might even be strongly apprehensive that her services would very shortly be dispensed with. And Doña Beatriz probably needed time to recover from the effects of her journey, and would make her appearance when there was less likelihood of a fastidious nature being slightly, if unavoidably, revolted.

For Lisa couldn't help remembering that it was all over Dr. Fernandez' expensive, light grey, superbly tailored suit that Gia had been violently sick, and she wondered whether he was holding that against her, Lisa. Although, as a doctor, that was one aspect of the matter that shouldn't greatly trouble him.

When she saw him again, late in the afternoon, he was wearing fine black slacks, and a silk shirt open at the neck. He looked composed and fresh, as if he had enjoyed a good lunch in the company of Doña Beatriz, indulged in the usual brief *siesta* — although sometimes it is not so brief, when the weather is very warm — looked upon by most Spaniards as an essential part of their organized day, and ready to be a little less hostile than his whole attitude had proclaimed him to be that morning. Having satisfied himself that Gia's temperature was normal, that she had enjoyed a good sleep, and was feeling hungry, he perched himself on the end of the bed and looked at Lisa. She even gathered that he was willing to listen to some sort of an explanation.

"That young man who was with you when we arrived this morning." He produced his cigarette-case, and then remembered where he was and put it away again. "Is he a particular friend of yours?"

Lisa, who was feeling stiff from much sitting, and had scarcely touched the tray that had been brought to her while the others were at lunch, returned his look vaguely.

"Particular friend? No. No, of course not. He was only an occasional visitor at the Hamilton-Traceys."

"The Hamilton-Traceys?"

"My last employers."

"Oh, yes!" His indescribably lustrous black eyes were studying her, but with an expression so unrevealing that she could have no idea what he was thinking. "And this young man met you at the Hamilton-Traceys, and came here because he hoped to see you again?"

She looked first amazed, and then shocked.

"See *me*? The governess! . . . Nursery-governess, I should say." She pushed her fair hair wearily back from her brow. "If you knew Mrs. Hamilton-Tracey you wouldn't ask such a question as that! I don't suppose I exchanged two words with Peter Hamilton-Tracey during the whole of the time I lived with the family, and even those two words were forgotten by him when he ran into me on the sands a few days ago. It is purely by accident that he is holidaying here."

"I see." But the black eyes seemed to hold such a cool tinge of doubt that they incensed her, and behind the doubt was that curious, blank wall of reserve that affected even the tones of his voice, so that at moments it had a strangely lifeless quality. "But you did run into him fairly regularly since?"

"We have met in the early mornings. I suppose it's not unnatural, under the circumstances."

"Compatriots, you mean?" She thought his lip curled a little. "Well, perhaps not. . . . And you are very young. You probably feel the need for companionship. But if you're already feeling homesick it's hardly a good sign. Do you like it here?"

"I love it. I told you I love San Cecilio."

"But this is not San Cecilio. This is rather an isolated spot."

'Nevertheless, I do love it. I think it's beautiful."

He nodded so slightly that she didn't know whether he agreed with her or not, and then he stood up and started pacing very quietly about the room. He picked up Gia's beach-wrap which still lay across the back of a chair, and examined it idly; then he peered at the toe of one of the slippers that peeped from the end of the bed, and finally caught sight of the little volume of English poetry which was actually Lisa's, but which she had given to Gia, and which now lay on the dressing-table top, and glanced through it with a temporarily averted attention. Then he thrust his hands in his pockets and turned and stared once more at Lisa.

'I understood you had few friends, and I certainly didn't expect you to run into one — quite literally! — so soon."

Lisa endeavored to convince him.

"Mr. Hamilton-Tracey is *not* a friend of mine. I know practically nothing about him."

"But you will continue to meet him while he is here?"

"I — I may, if — if you have no objections?"

She sounded so weary suddenly that he couldn't help noticing it, and when she once more pushed back her hair from her forehead as if the weight of it oppressed her his eyes narrowed.

"How long have you been siting there beside the bed?" he asked.

"Since this morning. You told me to do so, and in any case I wouldn't have dreamed of leaving Gia."

57

"And you had no breakfast, I suppose?"

"No, but it didn't matter. We usually visit the beach before breakfast."

"Did you have any lunch?"

"Señora Cortina brought me a tray."

"Did you eat what was brought to you on a tray?"

But as both pairs of eyes became glued as if the result of some mesmeric attraction to the tray that was not quite hidden away behind the window curtains on the window-seat, where she had sat for a short while while Gia was sunk in heavy slumber in the middle of the day, and it was plainly scarcely touched, she thought it best to say nothing.

"I think you had better go and have a bath and change, and then come downstairs and have a drink in the library," Dr. Fernandez said, with sudden incisiveness. "After which, of course, you will join us for dinner."

"Oh, but if you don't mind I'd rather not—join you for dinner, I mean. . . ." Lisa was beginning, when Gia awakened and stretched herself and reached forth a small, determined hand to clutch at her.

"Oh, no, you mustn't leave me!" the child cried, almost imperiously. "I don't *want* you to leave me!"

Her father surveyed her coldly.

"You are quite recovered," he said. "At any rate, you are recovered enough to be left alone, and Miss Waring has been cooped up here long enough. There is always the bell if you should require anything, and Señora Cortina can hear it in the kitchen."

Gia looked at him imploringly.

"I might be sick again."

"You won't," in the same cold tones.

"But I might! . . ." She began to whimper. 'And I am used to having Lisa with me! She

58

always has her own meals up here with me. . . ."

'What? In this bedroom?" He looked definitely shocked.

"No, no, in the sitting-room, which is next door," Lisa interposed hurriedly. She felt disturbed by the strange behavior of a man who could display so much concern for his child at one moment, and treat her almost with dislike the next. It strengthened her determination to stay with Gia. "And that, I thought, was a sensible arrangement, because it would be absurd to expect Señora Cortina to behave towards us as she would towards — well, you and Doña de Camponelli!

She didn't know quite why she included Doña de Camponelli, or why it seemed absolutely natural to link the two of them together, but it did, and the name slipped out. She thought he frowned peculiarly for an instant, and then he returned rather curtly:

"Sensible or not, tonight you will depart from a custom you seem to have established. I will expect you downstairs in the library in half an hour."

"I'd honestly rather not."

"And I don't intend to argue the matter."

He turned away and Lisa stooped above the small figure in the bed to soothe her. But as she did so she heard him remark dryly from the doorway:

"She has no temperature, and if you leave her alone she will sleep. Sleep is more important to her than your presence just now, although you may prefer not to believe that."

She felt not so much amazed as indignant, because having more or less openly accused her of neglect that morning, this evening he was implying that she coddled her charge. It was so unfair that she wanted to call him back to protest.

But he was not the sort of man one ventured to call back for any purpose whatsoever — not when one was merely an employee, and a more or less unknown English girl! And not for the first time she wondered whether she mightn't have been wiser to have resisted the temptation to stay on in Spain — and the temptation, which had been so overwhelming, to see more of him! The more she saw of him, apparently, the keener was going to become her sense of inferiority, the conviction that they were worlds apart, and that it had been sheer audacity to think that even in odd moments he might look upon her as if that was not the case.

She felt that so strongly when she went downstairs to the library that it was like an aura of foreboding that moved with her.

The library contained the Tintoretto and the Greek bronze. It was also a particularly attractive room at that hour of the day, with the last echo of sunset making an arresting loveliness of the sky outside the windows, and the swinging bronze lamps glowing like mellow moons in the room itself. The walls were starkly white, and there was a great deal of old oak across which the light fell softly. Spanish chests discovered a richness and a patina that fascinated Lisa, crimson silk curtains and velvet cushions were almost sensuously colorful, and silver candlesticks and copper bowls shone out of shadowy corners.

There were also a great many flowers, which Señora Cortina had arranged with a good deal of skill.

Doña Beatriz was lying back comfortably in a deep chair when Lisa entered. She was wearing her favorite black — which, incidentally, is a favorite with most Spanish women of good family, whether sophisticated or otherwise, as

Lisa discovered after only a very brief stay in in the country — and she was looking supremely elegant. Her perfume, which was French, and not Spanish, overlaid sharply the milder perfume of the massed red roses in the room.

"You feel quite easy about leaving your patient alone?" she inquired almost indolently of Lisa, as the girl moved into the rays of light from the gently swaying lamps, and it could be seen that she had changed into a simple little cocktail-type dress of misty-blue georgette.

Lisa felt almost taken aback for a moment by the studied coolness — even insolence — of the inquiry, and a ready reply would not rise to her lips. She was still feeling oddly strained after her long, confined day, and not even a bath had restored her mental alertness. And the fact that she was still in need of a good square meal made her seem hopelessly vulnerable just then.

But, surprisingly, Dr. Fernandez came quickly to her rescue. He lifted a decanter and poured sherry into a wineglass, and put it into her hand, and then her into a chair. He didn't smile at her, but his voice was quite gentle as he said, as if Doña Beatriz had said nothing at all:

"You shouldn't attempt to do a job of nursing on an empty stomach. It isn't fair to the patient, and it's certainly not fair to yourself."

Lisa heard herself stammering:
"No, I — I suppose not. . . ."
And then Doña Beatriz cut in:
"I don't suppose Miss Waring knows very much about nursing, Julio — she's too young! That's where your Miss Grimthorpe, though so offensive to look at, was in some ways more useful. She had trained properly for the job of looking after children, and she was of course thoroughly reliable." The inference here was so obvious that even the man frowned. "Did your training include any nursing, Miss Waring?"

Lisa had to admit that her training had been very brief, but reasonably comprehensive. She had been so anxious to start earning money that she hadn't dared to linger over the task of preparing herself, believing that all her instincts were the instincts that ultimately made for success when dealing with the young. And, so far as the young themselves were concerned, she had not so far proved that her instincts were at fault.

But she didn't say all this to Doña Beatriz. She merely explained about the brevity of her training, and watched the slow look of satisfaction dawn in the other's face.

"Then it *was* a little impetuous of you, Julio, to say the least, when you engaged Miss Waring!" the Spanish woman remarked. "And it could explain the unfortunate happening of this morning. Miss Waring isn't quite alive— not, shall we say, *sufficiently* alive to the responsibilities of her position as yet. But for your timely arrival on the scene anything might have happened to Gia!"

"I don't think so," Dr. Fernandez said, in a cool, almost a clipped tone, and his frown certainly didn't diminish. "It was never my opinion that Gia was in any actual danger, and she has admitted that she made short work of the contents of a box of confectionery — rather an outsize box for one as small as she is! — which you sent her only a few days ago. It was extremely generous of you, but Gia has a natural passion for sweet things, and the young are not particularly abstemious when it comes to anything they enjoy."

As a vexed expression flitted across Doña Beatriz's face, and she looked as if she was about to say something, he spoke quickly, cutting short any defence of herself she was about to make.

"I asked Señora Cortina to put forward the evening meal, as Miss Waring has had practically nothing to eat all day, and I think I hear movements in the dining-room now," he said suavely. "Shall we go in before the gong starts to wake up Gia, if she's asleep?"

During the meal — which was very definitely one of Señora Cortina's best, in spite of the request to hurry her culinary arrangements — Lisa was glad that the other two seemed to get back on a more harmonious footing. She had been surprised by the doctor's somewhat abrupt championship of herself, but she would have been uneasy if it had driven a wedge into the smooth companionship of this handsome pair who were in so many ways amazingly suited to one another. For Doña Beatriz was not the type to brook wedges being driven into any plans of her own. As it was, she was barely able to conceal the antipathy she felt for the English girl, and that antipathy would have increased if the English girl had been the cause of any strained relations between herself and the dark, determined doctor. And antipathy can be dangerous.

But, as the meal proceeded, delicious course following delicious course, the complacent calm of the dining-room seemed to fall like balm upon the spirits of each, and they discussed many things that could not possibly interest Lisa, content to be allowed to get quietly on with her own meal.

She had very little appetite, but the way to avoid attention was, she realized, to do as much justice as she could to the various savory helpings placed in front of her, and when at last coffee was served the only direct notice she received from her employer came her way.

"You did very well," he said quietly as she refused a liqueur. "Don't try starving yourself in future!"

Afterwards, in the big glassed-in verandah that opened on to the patio, Doña Beatriz seemed to regard her with more favor, also, and she even asked her a few questions about her life in England.

"If you're fond of foreign travel," she said, "and you prove yourself completely satisfactory while you are here" — with a meaning little pause to let this sink in — "I am almost certain I can help you to find another position that might take you even farther afield when the time arrives for Gia to go to school. I have a wide circle of friends, and a great many of them travel a good deal, and with young families help is always needed. Your time here will soon pass, and it might be as well if I begin to make inquiries with a view to obtaining for you some further employment."

"You are very kind," Lisa said, sitting still and pale as a moth in the gloom of the wide verandah, although the light of the rising moon made a splendor of her soft gold hair.

"Don't you think it's a little early to talk about finding Miss Waring further employment?" Dr. Fernandez inquired, staring at the tip of the cigarette he had just lighted. "Gia hasn't gone to school yet, and until she is reasonably fit I shall not make any definite plans for her to do so."

Doña Beatriz's eyebrows arched.

"But I understood they *were* made! We talked the whole thing over."

Lisa stood up.

"Do you mind if I go to bed?" she asked. "And I would like to make absolutely certain that Gia is quite all right."

The doctor nodded casually.

'You will find that she is fast asleep, and in the morning will be much as usual. But you probably do feel tired, and of course we don't mind if you go to bed."

It was a politely careless dismissal, and it made something deep inside her feel very lonely and isolated just then. But she took herself to task as she went up the wide staircase. Her employer was considerate in his detached, impersonal fashion, and if it was impersonal that was not his fault. A governess was, after all, a governess — and he had Doña Beatriz, with whom he no doubt wanted to be alone.

But it would have been impossible for anyone to swear to it that he wanted to be alone with Doña Beatriz. Lovely as the Spanish woman was — his own enchanting fellow-countrywoman! — exotic as she appeared in her black dress, and alluring as those brilliant dark eyes of her were, there was, at frequent intervals, a something in their relationship—just a touch, of ill-concealed impatience on his part, a quick, resentful look on hers, that could have given rise to doubts if anyone had been attempting to speculate.

And Lisa found herself speculating frequently. She felt that it was all-important, even though it was no concern of hers whatsoever, that she should find out what their attitude to one another was. And whether that strange aloofness at time, that almost monastic withdrawal — as if women had no real place in Julio Fernandez's scheme of things, because in spite of being rather more attractive physically than most men he had no real need of women, or the softer side of life— was merely a screen behind which he hid. Or whether there was nothing to hide.

CHAPTER SEVEN

THE NEXT morning he and Doña Beatriz
went off together in his big white car, and they
didn't return until lunchtime. Gia, as he had
predicted, was quite herself again, but Lisa
decided to run no risks with her, and they spent
the morning extremely quietly within the confines
and the shade of the tangled garden by the sea.

Just before lunch-time Peter Hamilton-Tracey
made his appearance, and Lisa wished he hadn't.
He said he wanted to be sure she hadn't been
fired on the spot as the result of what had
happened before breakfast the day before, and
expressed his opinion that an enormous amount
of fuss had been made about nothing at all.

"If you need me to support you on any occasion
just call upon me when, and at any time, you
please," he said, looking at her as if he found
doing so a most pleasing occupation. "If you ask
me, looking after other people's children is a
thankless task, and that goes for my brother's
offspring as well. You must have had a brute
of a time with them, particularly as my sister-in-
law isn't the easiest type in the world to get on
with."

"Your brother was very kind," Lisa admitted,
realizing at this distance of time that he had
been extremely kind on occasion. "I never found
him difficult to get on with."

Peter smiled.

"I shouldn't think many men would find it
possible to be anything other than kind in their
dealings with you," he told her, thinking that she
looked like a delicate sprite in her pastel-tinted
sun-suit, the most modest sun-suit he had ever
seen any young woman wear, and with her hair of
palest wedding-ring gold, and her large, clear,

slightly wistful eyes. Looking into them he decided that they were the grey of the fires that burned in English woodlands in the autumn, and her mouth was positively flower-like. He wondered why she had made so little impression on him when they had met before, and then came to the conclusion that it was because she had kept so skilfully out of his way. She was not the type to thrust herself on anybody's vision. "Even that doctor chappie you work for now looked the least little bit irritated when his lovely lady friend — and, by Jove, she is lovely, isn't she? — kept sailing into you for neglecting your charge. And of course you weren't neglecting your charge!"

He repeated this when the others drove up, and Doña Beatrice looked at him with a peculiar kind of half-inviting smile in her eyes.

"I came to inquire how Gia was doing today," he said, as Gia's father looked at him without a suspicion of a smile in his eyes. " I understand she's more or less fully recovered." And as Gia's laughter reached them from the other side of the house, where she was helping Señora Cortina's elderly husband sweep out the patio with a stiff birch broom, it was impossibl for anyone to deny this.

"Children recover quickly from upsets," was all the doctor remarked.

"Stomach upsets, yes," Peter agreed. "But not frights like getting out of their depth, or anything of that sort," looking Fernandez straight in the eyes, as if he at least had not forgotten Lisa's humiliation of the day before. "And as Gia can't swim a foot without being supported there was never any question of her getting out of her depth, and certainly no question of Lisa neglecting her."

"We are reasonably convinced now that Gia had been eating too many chocolates of a rather too excellent quality," Dona Beatriz informed him, a little dryly.

Peter looked relieved.

"Well, that lets you out, Lisa!" he exclaimed. "And, incidentally, me, as well!" he added. "I don't like being accused of permitting a small kid to run into danger." He sounded the least little bit aggressive.

Doña Beatriz smiled at him this time as if it was her particular aim to soothe him.

"In the heat of the moment one is apt to be unjust, perhaps," she admitted, "and naturally Dr. Fernandez has a great deal of concern for an only child. It should not be too difficult to understand."

But the Englishman didn't look impressed.

"I was just commiserating with Lisa on being forced continually to look after other people's children," he confessed, "my own brother's amongst them! It must be a pretty thankless task sometimes."

"No doubt," Doña Beatriz agreed. "But, in that case, the answer surely is that Miss Waring must get married and have some of her own?" with an archness that brought a flame of color to Lisa's cheeks, and caused Peter to look amused. "If you are a friend of Miss Waring's, Mr. Hamilton-Tracey," the Spanish woman went on, as if an idea had only just occurred to her, "you must come and have lunch with us sometimes, or perhaps dinner one night would suit you better? Don't you agree with me, Julio, that if Miss Waring and Mr. Hamilton-Tracey are old friends they simply must see something of one another sometimes, apart from odd meetings on the beach?"

Dr. Fernandez said formally that he understood that Miss Waring and Mr. Hamilton-Tracey scarcely knew one another, but no doubt when two people of the same nationality met abroad they experienced a desire to pursue the acquaintance. It was fairly easily understood. And then he added, even more formally, that he had no objection to Mr. Hamilton-Tracey lunching, or dining, at the villa; and Doña Beatriz seized upon this permission to issue an invitation to lunch for that very day.

But because he could not possibly have failed to sense the cool and quite definite reluctance behind the doctor's seconding of Doña Beatriz's invitation, Peter declined — with thanks, however, and a particularly attractive smile for the Spanish woman, who said that in that case he simply must come to dinner one evening. And then she vanished into the house to prepare herself for lunch, and the doctor followed her, and Lisa made it clear, by means of a slightly agonized look, that she wished Peter to execute a prompt disappearance also. He smiled at her — a much more warm and understanding smile than the one he had directed at Doña Beatriz — and waved a hand, and turned on his heel.

"But you'll be seeing me!" he promised. "For, after all, we *are* two people of the same nationality abroad, and I, for one, definitely wish to pursue the acquaintance!"

And with a still more impish smile he climbed into a decrepit sports car he had left outside the gate, and roared off in it.

The following morning Dr. Fernandez drove Doña Beatriz, Gia, and Lisa into San Cecilio. Doña Beatriz slipped gracefully into the seat beside the driving-seat as if it was hers by right, and Gia and Lisa were relegated to the back. The outing was because Doña Beatriz had decided that Gia needed new sandals for the beach, and apparently it was a self-imposed task for her to see to it that the child's wardrobe was constantly replenished. (Hence, Lisa thought, the lovely almost too-smart outfits the doctor's plain little daughter possessed)!

She herself had no idea of accompanying them until the doctor saw her waiting at the side of the white, dusty road, within a few yards of the villa, for the bus that would presently make its leisurely appearance and deposit her also in San Cecilio. The big white car drew in towards the verge and pulled up with rather a sudden application of brakes, and Julio Fernandez leaned frowningly from his window.

'Why are you waiting there, Miss Waring?" he asked.

"I'm waiting for the bus," she explained. "I have some shopping to do for Señora Cortina— at least," she added, rather hurriedly, "something was suddenly discovered to be in rather short supply, and I offered to fetch it."

He reached in behind him and held open the rear door.

"Get in," he said curtly.

She hesitated, aware that Doña Beatriz was biting her scarlet lower lip, as if the temporary halt — or more probably the cause! — annoyed her.

"It's quite all right," she said, with nervous diffidence. "The bus will be along in a minute, and——"

"Get in!" the doctor repeated, his voice not merely curt this time, but impatient.

Lisa clambered in, assisted by Gia's eager hands, and the child's shrill voice declared delightedly:

"We'll have ice creams at Antonio's Parlour! I was simply hating not having you, and now it's going to be *fun*!"

Dr. Fernandez asked over his shoulder:

"Do you normally do Señora Cortina's shopping for her, Miss Waring?"

"Oh, no," she answered at once. "Only some-times — if she runs out of something. Normally everything's delivered."

"I see." But she thought that the "I see" was sceptical, as if he doubted the smooth running of his holiday household while he was away, and surmised that there might be a considerable amount of wasted time — or, worse still, neglected duty! — when he was not there to keep an eye on things, with Señora Cortina making use of his highly-paid governess to fetch and carry for her, and the highly-paid governess looking upon visits to the little local town as a respite from governing.

She felt so guilty because she had involved Señora Cortina — it didn't matter that she her-self was to be so frequently suspect! — that she was very quiet and anxious to escape as quickly as possible when they reached the town, and Gia's insistence that they should visit Antonio's Parlour before they did anything else met with discourage-ment from her as well as Doña Beatriz.

"No, darling, you're going to have some new shoes bought for you, and Doña Beatriz is waiting to take you to the shoe-shop," she said hurriedly, before Doña Beatriz herself could interpose a few rather clipped remarks. "There'll be heaps of other times when we can visit Antonio's Parlour."

"If you want ice cream, we'll have it at the hotel," Doña Beatriz took her firmly by the hand, and started to lead her from the parking-place. Lisa remembered her shopping basket, and recovered it hastily from the back of the car, and Dr. Fernandez stood watching her with rather an odd — even a quizzical — expression on his face.

"And now where exactly are you making for?" he asked.

She told him what it was she had to collect, and he slipped his ignition key into his pocket and turned to walk beside her.

"I'll come with you," he said. "You might lose your way. Some of these narrow streets are not precisely the streets you ought to traverse, and I've no interest in children's shoes, anyway." He walked with an easy grace at her side — much as she remembered him walking on the first and only night they had been alone together — and although it was almost painfully pleasant to have him doing so, it also filled her with a great deal of agitation. She thought of Doña Beatriz, and the annoyance such an attention would undoubtedly fill her with, and the various ways in which she might seek to put Lisa in her place afterwards. She also felt concerned because, although it was probably true that he had no interest in children's shoes, there were almost certainly other ways in which the doctor might have passed his morning, which would have been much more to his taste than making certain she didn't get side-tracked down a wrong turning.

She felt all this so strongly that there was a little frown of anxiety between her brows as they made their way to the shop where she was to execute several purchases, and although he talked to her casually, her answers were abstracted. When she reached the shop she simply tore in and was successful in getting someone to attend to her immediately — a most unusual happening in a country where everybody believed that there was little point in hurrying over anything — and returned to the sidewalk with the anxious expression still on her face, and the words of apology on her lips.

"I do hope I didn't keep you waiting! . . . Although there wasn't the slightest need for you to wait for me."

He smiled, his velvety dark eyes surveying her upturned face rather carefully.

"You sound as if you're anxious to get rid of me," he said. And then enlightenment dawned on him. "You weren't proposing to meet someone in San Cecilio, were you?"

They both knew he meant Peter Hamilton-Tracey, but the suggestion filled Lisa with honest surprise.

"Of course I wasn't." She sounded indignant. "I don't arrange to meet people in your time, Dr. Fernandez!"

"No?" It was almost as if the light, and exquisitely delicate flush that rose to her cheeks intrigued him, or the spark of indignation in her grey eyes fascinated him for some odd reason. He went on gazing down at her, while they stood within a foot of one another on the pavement. "Then why would you have preferred that I didn't accompany you here? Why have you been so silent, with a little forbidding frown between your brows, as if you were trying to think up some excuse for sending me about my business?"

She was silent for a moment, and then she answered truthfully:

"I was thinking of Doña Beatriz — that she would no doubt have preferred it if you had accompanied *her*! And I was also thinking that you must be bored, and it was a pity you saw me waiting for the bus."

He took her by the arm and turned her back along the street.

"I am not in the least bored," he told her, in a quiet voice that was completely uninformative, "and any time I can give you a lift and save you waiting for the bus I will willingly do so! As for Doña Beatriz" — he paused — "it was her idea that Gia wanted new shoes, and she knows my views on shopping expeditions very well." Apparently shopping in a grocer's in a side

73

street of the quaint little town didn't come into the same category! "And she's probably enjoying herself, anyway, adding all sorts of unwanted items to Gia's wardrobe."

Suddenly he smiled down at her, and it was a smile that caused her heart to knock, just as the fact that he retained a light hold of her arm, and insisted on carrying her shopping basket for her, made something deep inside her feel light and grateful, and at the same time unstable.

"Let's stop here, shall we?" he suggested, and she saw that they had come to a halt beside an open-air cafe. This isn't 'Antonio's Parlour' — apparently the Mecca of my daughter's life when she comes to San Cecilio! — but we can have some coffee, unless you really would prefer ice cream? Have you, like Gia, an insatiable appetite for ice cream?"

She laughed, a little uncertainly.

"Of course not! Although I'll admit that, on the few occasions that we've come here, we have been inclined to make tracks for Antonio's. But that's probably because he does serve excellent ice cream."

"And you're not very much older — in spirit, shall we say? — than Gia, in some ways," he remarked, a trifle obscurely, and pulled forward a gaily painted chair for her, at a table with a check cloth.

The coffee was excellent, and Lisa enjoyed it— particularly as the outlook was across an open square shaded by green trees overhanging sharply contrasting high white walls. There was a narrow gap in one of the walls, and she could see at the end of a little tunnel-like passageway a dazzling blob of blue sea, and right in the middle of it was the graceful white curve of a yacht's sail.

Overhanging the white walls, in addition to the wide-spreading branches, were torrents of flaming growth, and painted doorways looked as if they guarded the interiors of exciting, and in some cases very old, dwellings, whose windows had the inevitable curly wrought-iron balconies attached to them, while little grilles let into the brickwork here and there gave the impression of watchful eyes.

The centre of the square was very placid, with sunshine falling in golden splashes, and people drifting leisurely to and fro in the enervating soft warmth. In the afternoon the heat would be too intense for that kind of perambulation, and the square would empty of everything save flies, and one or two unwanted taxi-cabs. In the evening it would be shadowy and cool, and late at night it would be transformed altogether by moonlight — a plaza of magic black and white guitar echoes floating on the still, sweet night air, a serenading voice stealing out of an intersecting alleyway, and the murmur of the sea a background to guarded footfalls and, perhaps, occasional laughter.

Spain! . . . Lisa felt, this morning, that it had all the color and the romance of the ages, and it was a color and romance that had got into her blood. The thought that depressed her was that soon — all too soon — she would have to get it out of her blood, and when that time arrived she would have to say a final good-bye to it all.

Watching her across the table, and the check cloth, her employer seemed intrigued by those revealing, and yet unrevealing, expressions on her face.

"You told me the other day that you still like San Cecilio," he said. "Is that one reason why you are apparently quite willing to perform errands for Señora Cortina when she finds herself in imminent danger of running out of something vital to her culinary needs?"

75

Lisa smiled.

"Señora Cortina is not really as careless as all that, and she's the most wonderful cook I've ever known. Now that I'm getting used to Spanish dishes I realize that more and more every day."

"And now that you are getting used to Spain, and the Spanish way of life, how do you feel about that?"

"I——" She looked at him for an instant, and then away. This was where she could betray herself, if she wasn't careful. "I think that it's a very colorful way of life, and very restful. Nobody ever hurries; nobody ever thinks that any single thing is important enough to receive prompt attention, and yet things do get done. Life itself is, I think, of tremendous importance to you Spanish people."

"Life, and love, and death!" he interposed, with a queer flickering of a smile in his dark eyes as he gazed at her. "Birth, love, and death — those are the main preoccupations. But, then, they are the main preoccupations of people all over the world. And the only difference with us Spaniards is that we like to dwell upon them, and accent the importance of them, in our daily life. Birth is natural, but it is also an exciting fulfilment. Love is something every woman hopes for, and with our women there is usually only one love. It is the result of the way in which they are brought up and prepared for marriage."

"But marriage doesn't necessarily mean love," she interjected.

"Doesn't it?" One of his dark eyebrows rose. "How would you know?"

"I don't know, of course, but . . . in Spain you arrange marriages, and one can't love to order?"

'No?" This time his eyes looked cool and amused by her confusion. "Yet so many of those marriages turn out to be a success that perhaps love is more like a plant one cares for deliberately, than a haphazard gathering of wild flowers. In any case, the wild flowers will fade sooner or later, whereas the plant might very well last out a lifetime."

She found herself so fascinated by the quiet, measured tones of his voice that, in spite of the amusement in his eyes, she stared straight into them. He said softly, after a moment:

"You agree with me?"

"No." She shook her head quite violently. "I know nothing about love, as you just implied, but I would prefer it to be a gathering of wild flowers instead of a plant that I would have to painstakingly persuade to grow! One gathers wild flowers when one is in a happy mood, and they are so perfect when you pick them — even the commonest varieties. And one never quite knows how a plant will develop, or what its blooms will be like, and — and, in any case, I'm no gardener!" she concluded, with such a burst of firmness and decisiveness, and such a determined setting of her soft lips and small chin, that he actually laughed aloud.

"Then for you we will recommend the gathering of wild flowers — perhaps the plucking of the one perfect rose in the garden! If you are lucky enough to find a garden to wander in where such a rose might be found!" He surveyed her with sudden gravity. "Would that suit you better?"

She looked down hastily into her nearly empty coffee cup, and he ordered the waiter to bring her another.

"No, no!" she said. "Won't the others be wondering where you are? I mustn't keep you."

"Never mind the others for the time being," he replied. He looked almost impatient. "I asked you a question. Would that suit you better?"

77

"The — the one rose . . .?" She felt the color stealing back into her cheeks as she lifted her eyes. "Yes — naturally!"

"And you wouldn't ever want to discard it?"

"Not once I'd found it," with an earnestness that got the better of her shyness as they steadily gazed at one another.

This time it was he who looked down into his coffee cup.

"Unhappily it is seldom that we find what we are looking for in this life," he commented.

Lisa studied the night-blackness of his hair, and the way it grew back from his excellently shaped forehead in that slight but intriguing Marie Stuart peak. Not for the first time, too, she marvelled at the length and thickness of his eyelashes, and her heart turned over at the strength and beauty of his mouth. It was almost too perfectly shaped a mouth, and too calm and composed.

She said quickly, before she properly realized what she was saying:

"You said that love is something every woman hopes for—every Spanish woman, that is! What about Spanish men? Don't they hope for it also?"

He lighted a cigarette with his slender, beautifully formed fingers, and when he was quite certain that it was alight he gazed at her through the faint, blue mist of cigarette smoke that crept between them.

"Men — men of any nationality — are different from women. It is their task to go forth into the world and wrest a living from some corner of it, in order to provide for the woman they eventually choose. At least, that was the old idea. And in Spain, today, it is much as it used to be. Our women are seldom the providers, and they do not take kindly to performing two sets of duties. In your country it is different, of course. . . . ."

"But — love?" she heard herself insisting, although she didn't quite know why she did so, or how she found the courage to do so when he was such a distant employer, who had only for the moment unbent to her.

He put back his head and followed the ascending spirals of smoke as they merged with the sunny air beneath the trees that overhung the café.

"Spanish men are preoccupied with loving rather than love," he answered, causing her slender brows to wrinkle. "With loving Life, and making certain that it is always spelled with a capital L . . . living it with zest! That is why they are so preoccupied with death, and why you find them challenging it in the bull-ring! Why bull-fights are as popular with us as football matches are with you! There is more danger in the bull-ring."

"And Spaniards love danger?"

"They love the element of danger — the flirting with death. And, besides, the more they wantonly risk their own lives, the brighter the eyes that watch them!"

"And that brings us back to love!"

"That brings you back to love," he said gently. "But then you are young, and naturally you are intrigued by the very thought of it. For myself, I am far too busy, usually, to think of it very much. . . . And I am many years older than you are. My experiences are in the past, and will remain there."

She felt as if she had been deliberately rebuffed, and the warm air grew a little less warm, the charm of the square less obvious.

"I really do think you should rejoin Doña Beatriz now," she said, collecting her handbag and shopping basket.

"Why?" He reached out to deprive her of the shopping basket. "Am I not permitted to sit here

in the sun if I wish?" and he surveyed her quizzically, and also as if he wondered at her abrupt
desire to move.

"You forget," she said, looking at a clock in
the window of a chemist's shop opposite, "that it
is getting on for lunch-time, and Doña Beatriz
said something about lunching at the hotel. She
will be expecting to meet you there. And I," she
added firmly, "have a bus to catch!"

"If the plan is to lunch at the hotel, then you
will lunch there with us."

"No," with an incisiveness in her clear, English
voice. "Señorita Cortina is waiting for the things
I bought this morning, and in any case I do not
expect to be entertained to lunch during working
hours—not by my employer! But if you would
like me to take Gia back with me I will do so."

"If you and Gia are going back, we will all go
back," he said a little curtly, rising. And then he
looked hard at her. "With your employer's permission, apparently, you would lunch during working
hours with anyone else who asked you?"

She looked up at him in surprise.

"No one else has asked me."

"Not this morning — no! But some other morning — yes? Mr. Peter Hamilton-Tracey, who
Beatriz insists is a very close friend of yours,
might ask you, and then you would approach
me for permission to do so?"

She felt herself flushing with a kind of anger
this time.

"Doña Beatriz has no right to insist that Mr.
Hamilton-Tracey is a close friend of mine, because
it is not true."

"But, nevertheless, he might ask you to lunch
with him one day. And what then?" he wanted to
know.

She turned away, vaguely irritated because he
insisted on carrying the shopping basket, and not
only did it strike her as far below his dignity to

do so, but with it she might have made a hurried escape.

"We will wait until I receive such an invitation, and then I will let you know what my reactions to it are," she told him, with such prim demureness that his eyes raked her face almost curiously.

And then they ran straight into Doña Beatriz, dragging a sadly deflated-looking Gia by the hand, and, there was no doubt about it, Doña Beatriz was annoyed.

"We have been hunting for you everywhere, Julio!" she informed him, surveying him with a strong hint of displeasure. "And we have been standing beside the car in the car-park for at least half an hour, expecting you to rejoin us! Gia is quite worn out with wandering about the streets."

"Then you should have gone to the hotel and had your ice," Julio returned, without even wilting under the displeasure.

She regarded him with a hurt look this time.

"But naturally we thought *you* would accompany us to the hotel, and I am amazed that you are still in the company of Miss Waring!"

"There is no reason why you should be amazed." His voice was cool as the first flake of wintry snow when it fell in the Gudarrama that looked down on his home in Madrid. "Miss Waring could hardly be expected to return in the bus with this heavy shopping basket" — actually, the contents of it were quite light — "and I have been doing my best to persuade her to have lunch with us. But she insists on going back to the villa, so there is nothing for it but that we must all go back! And perhaps that's just as well since Señora Cortina is expecting us."

"Really!" Doña Beatriz exclaimed, as if exasperation was running away with her. "You know very well that we arranged to have lunch——"

"I don't think we did." They had reached the car-park, and he had deposited the shopping basket in the back of the car. "You *talked* about lunch on the way here, but that is as far as we got. And unless I leave strict instructions behind me I don't like to disappoint the efforts of people I employ."

Doña Beatriz tightened her lips and got in beside him, and Gia slipped a hand into Lisa's arm and hugged it when they were together once more on the roomy back seat.

"It's been a *horrid* morning!" the child confided in a whisper to the English girl. "She" — Lisa said "Ssh!" in a warning whisper because the "she" was so loud, and Gia looked impish for a moment, and then developed an even more penetrating whisper — "*she* said I ought to be wearing gloves when I went out with Papa, and as well as new sandals I've got new gloves!" She exhibited them. "They're hot, and I don't like the feel of them! Can I take them off?"

But after an anxious glance at Doña Beatriz's rigid back Lisa decided to advise her to keep them on. For that morning, at least.

"And I didn't even have an ice cream!" Gia lamented. "It wouldn't have been so bad if I'd had an ice cream!"

CHAPTER EIGHT

THREE NIGHTS later Peter Hamilton-Tracey accepted an invitation to dinner, and since Doña Beatriz was responsible for the invitation, and it was issued through her. the young man behaved towards her as if she was a legitimate hostess in her own house, and not simply a guest in the house of a man to whom — so far — she was not even engaged to be married.

But to Peter it seemed clear enough that she was fairly certain of what was going to happen to her one day. She was going to become the second wife of Dr. Julio Fernandez, or be exceedingly surprised herself. Already, in her attitude towards him, there was the easy comradeship of a woman who was upon the very verge of becoming a wife. She teased him, gently — rallied him, with the same sort of gentleness, upon all sorts of subjects. But behind the gentleness, there was an inflexible firmness, a suave determination to carry the point whenever it was really necessary; and if this determination was wrapped up in the Spanish woman's desire, at all costs, to please her man, and recognize his right to exert authority in his own home, nevertheless it was there beneath the wrappings, and to Peter it was a little sinister.

He felt that he would have hated to be married to such a woman himself, for in time her will could become all-powerful. And although she was extremely attractive, dressed beautifully, looked the part of a successful doctor's wife — or would do when she became one! — and was born to be a perfect hostess, he still felt that someone less endowed with many attributes would suit him better. And might even suit a very successful doctor better!

Not that Dr. Fernandez conveyed the impression that his quiet brilliance would be easily overlaid, or his authority flouted if he really chose to exert it. On the contrary, there were moments when a note of incisiveness in his voice had the effect of causing Doña Beatriz to look temporarily at a loss, and when a certain cool flash in his eyes actually reduced her to silence. There were even times when he looked a little bored — when, for instance, the subject of his daughter was dragged into the conversation rather more than he obviously approved, and Doña Beatriz became impassioned about the advisability of sending only children to school, preferably a really sound boarding-school, as soon as they were old enough, in order to avoid the evils of introspectiveness and slight spoiling.

"But then Julio knows my views on this subject, as I have expressed them very often," she remarked, shaking her head with doubtful indulgence as she surveyed the doctor, and Peter could have sworn that impatience suddenly seethed in him , and that it was rather more than boredom that caused him to observe with an empty expression:

"I am sure Mr. Hamilton-Tracey is not interested in the ubringing of only children as a subject for dinner-table conversation, however absorbing the topic may be to us!"

And then he rose and led the way out into the veranda, where coffee was always served.

Doña Beatriz was too skilled at masking her reactions to most things to reveal what she felt on this occasion, and within a few moments the host was being carefully attentive to her, and the little irruption on the placid pool of their relationship had passed. But mostly it was a placid relationship, and this fact in itself struck Peter Hamilton-Tracey as strange. Warm-blooded people like the Spanish didn't normally indulge in placid relationships, and there was a kind of slumbrous fire in Doña Beatriz's fine dark eyes at times — especially when she sat looking for any length of time at Julio Fernandez — and for all the control he exercised over his own features they were not always mask-like. The mouth was too human, the eyes too full of depths for that. And Lisa had discovered that he could laugh quite gaily on occasion, and his reactions were sometimes surprising.

There could be plenty of warm blood flowing through his veins if he hadn't perhaps discovered that warm blood was safer when it was carefully damned and regulated.

Lisa was very quiet during dinner while Peter was there, and he himself received the impression that she had formed the habit of listening to the voices of the other two. Although Doña Beatriz was charming to him, she never deliberately included Lisa in the conversation. And apart from making certain that she was never neglected her employer addressed little of his actual conversation to her. He seemed content to send quiet, reflective glances in her direction occasionally, and then to look a little curiously at Peter, as if he was trying to decide something in his mind.

After dinner the two younger people wandered out into the garden — Peter thinking up an excuse that was not too transparent, although it involved catching a glimpse of the sea from the higher part of the grounds, and witnessing the effect of moonlight on the white beach that lay below. Doña Beatriz smiled somewhat oddly when they had disappeared, and looked round and up at Julio, who was standing staring out into the patio.

"These English are rather obvious, don't you agree?" she said, the smile changing to the corners of her scarlet mouth. "We do not need to be told why those two have gone out there together into the night, and if Miss Waring had been brought up as our Spanish girls are brought up she would at least have displayed a certain diffidence before accepting such an invitation as that!"

"What sort of an invitation?" Julio inquired, staring rather frowningly at the tip of his shoe instead of the moonlit patio.

"Oh, my dear Julio!" She reached out and patted his arm and laughed. "Young lovers are young lovers the world over, only in England it does not follow that they have to marry because they make a little light love! Miss Waring likes to pretend she doesn't know Peter Hamilton-Tracey very well, but it is obvious they are greatly attracted to one another, otherwise he would not have come here tonight, and she would not seize upon the first opportunity to be alone with him!"

"I didn't notice any excessive enthusiasm on her part to be alone with him," the man remarked.

Again the soft, amused laughter reached him out of the dimness.

"But that is because you are not particularly interested in her, and therefore not very observant where she is concerned!"

"Perhaps not," he agreed, and his voice sounded short as he turned away. "Beatriz, I would like you to understand that Gia will go to school when I decide that the time is ripe!"

"Of course." Her voice was soothing as the murmur of the sea as it slapped gently on the beach below them. "And in the meantime you will permit me to go ahead with inquiries and preparations? There is a dental appointment that simply must be kept in a week or so's time, and that will necessitate a return to Madrid for Gia. I hardly think it necessary for Miss Waring to accompany her, and while the child is with us I can see about fittings for new clothes and so forth. That will probably take some time, but she can stay with me at my flat if you do not wish to have her with you."

All at once he turned and looked at her. His eyes were more enigmatic than she had ever known before, and it disturbed her.

"Is there any good reason why I should object to having Gia with me?"

"My dear Julio," she began again, "there is the excellent reason that yours is a bachelor flat, and if Miss Waring remains here there will be no one to look after her — no woman, that is."

"Then why should not Miss Waring accompany her?"

This time she shook her head at him.

"Have I not just said that yours is a bachelor flat? Miss Grimthorpe was a different proposition entirely from Miss Waring — although you may not realize it, since, as I remarked, you probably hardly notice her! — but you could hardly, without a housekeeper, or some other woman in the house, take her to live with you."

"Then why should I not install the pair of them in an hotel?"

There was a curious stubborn note in his voice that surprised her, and she rose suddenly, and very gratefully, and went towards him.

"Julio!..." There was a soft rebuke in her voice as she laid hold of his sleeve. "Why may not I do all that I can to help you with Gia? Haven't I *always* done my best to help you with her?"

His night-dark, unrevealing eyes stared hard at her.

"You suggested that she should spend the summer here by the sea, as a preparation for the autumn, and now that she is here you want to take her away!"

"Only for a routine check on her teeth, and so forth. And also I am not sure that Miss Waring is the right type of person to be left alone with her. She is too young. This friend of hers, Peter Hamilton-Tracey, is too close!"

"He will be going away soon."

She shrugged, her white shoulders gleaming in the moon-beams.

"There will be others. She is that sort. A moth to the candle! . . . And do you forget what happened to Gia's mother? Do you forget all that you had to live through at one time, and do you wish to have to repeat such a performance through your daughter?"

"Don't!" he said, and his voice sounded almost violent.

But she clung tenaciously to his sleeve.

"Julio, *mi querido*," she said softly, "I do not wish to wound you, but you must not forget that Gia's upbringing is important — far more important than it would be, say, if she were your daughter and mine!" moving imperceptibly nearer to him. "If Gia were *our* daughter," still more softly, "there would be little or no danger, and a good deal of latitude would be permissible. But Gia is her *mother's* daughter — apart from the fact, of course, that she will never have her mother's looks! — and we must safeguard her, you and I. And you know that your interests, and the interests of Gia, are entirely my interests."

To her acute disappointment he moved away, and he did so without even seeming to notice that touch on his sleeve. His voice sounded moody when he reached the far end of the veranda.

"Perhaps you are right, but I do not think you know Miss Waring sufficiently well to criticize her behavior with men friends."

"No?" All at once her eyes narrowed, and their expression was like something that had been abruptly alerted. "Well, perhaps you are right there, but I am also not sufficiently interested in Miss Waring to care one way or the other — save that anyone who arouses doubt is not an ideal person to have charge of a child like Gia! In any case, I told you in the beginning that she is the very last person I would have chosen for myself — an unknown young woman on a pathetic little holiday that failed to produce any of the things she had hoped for, and with probably not even the means to get back to her own country! *That* was why she seized on your offer of a position with Gia! You were very unwise not to take up the references she provided you with."

"Whether I was unwise or not, I do not think that anything can be gained by discussing her in this manner at the moment," he said, and all at once his voice had that cool note of ice in it that always vaguely frightened her. He walked back along the length of the veranda until he came face to face with her again. "You can have Gia to stay with you in Madrid if you wish, Beatriz, and Miss Waring can await her return here. There are a good many weeks yet before the summer is ended, and you were right at least about sea air for Gia. She has thrived quite noticeably here on the coast."

"But only because the sea air *is* so good! You mustn't get it into your head that it is because of some magic Miss Waring possesses." She smiled at him as if she was willing to humor him quite a long way, but false notions about an English governess must be firmly eradicated. And then, because she had herself been put in her place — even politely warned about excessive interference — she added comfortably: "But don't worry about Miss Waring. If she behaves herself I will find her that other job I promised her, and your sense of responsibility where she is concerned will be satisfied. There will be no need for you to develop a conscience when the time comes for her to leave Gia."

"I am not in the least likely to develop a conscience about Miss Waring," he replied, and from the tone of his reply it was impossible to gather what exactly he meant by it. And then, as if his conscience where Beatriz was concerned suddenly troubled him, he looked down at her and smiled apologetically. "It is very good of you, Beatriz, to trouble yourself as much as you do about me and my affairs, and particularly about Gia. You do know I'm grateful, don't you?"

"You don't have to be grateful," she told him, taking his arm quite firmly and leading him out into the moonlit garden. "You and your affairs have long been one of my main preoccupations, and I don't think you need me to assure you that is the way it always will be!"

For one instant, as she put back her sleek red head and looked up at him, he read something like reproach in her eyes, and he felt, as he had felt often before, definitely uneasy. For was that the way he wanted it to be — always? And, if he did, ought not something warmer than gratitude to be offered her?

He was certain she was growing a little tired of gratitude, and nothing else!

In a far corner of the garden Peter Hamilton-Tracey was saying awkwardly to Lisa:

"You know, I don't want to make things uncomfortable for you, but it is an opportunity to see you if I'm invited here to the house! At the same time I'm pretty certain your boss doesn't enjoy seeing me at his dinner table, and that Doña Beatriz is inexplicable. She seems very anxious to throw you and I together, but she doesn't strike me as being particularly friendly towards you. Would you prefer it if I didn't come here again?"

"Of course not," Lisa answered. They were standing before a low wall smothered in sweet-smelling growth, and before them the sea was a pathway of magic, with the umbrella pines like black silhouettes overhanging the water, and she was so captivated by the beauty of it all that she wasn't really paying attention to what he was saying. "Why shouldn't we meet? At least . . ." And then she hesitated, recalling her employer's bleak expression at dinner, and she thought she knew what Peter was driving at. "You think that Doña Beatriz takes rather a lot on herself, and that Dr. Fernandez doesn't always approve? After all, I'm only a governess. I oughtn't to be dining with them at all."

"Nonsense." Peter took her cool bare arm, and led her away from the wall. "That wasn't what I meant at all!" He tried to explain. "Fernandez is strange and reticent, and it would be impossible to decide quite definitely how he feels about many things — his daughter amongst them! Doña Beatriz has probably got him very well weighed up, and in spite of the fact that he was obviously not at all keen to have me invited to the house she went on pressing her invitations. She keeps making you the pretext. . . . I don't want to make things awkward for you"

"You mean that she likes you, and — and Dr. Fernandez might be jealous?"

"No, I don't." He laughed. "I'm not as conceited as all that! But I don't think she likes you, and you need that job for the rest of the summer, and if you're to retain it we don't want Fernandez upset in any way. But you're entitled to a certain amount of free time, and there's no reason why we shouldn't spend some of it together."

"N-no, I supose not," she agreed doubtfully.

He gave her smooth elbow a little shake.

"Be your age, child! You need fun and games like anyone else, and the atmosphere of this place isn't exactly bubbling over with merriment. Doña Beatriz doesn't aprove of merriment, only Dior dresses, and looking ravishing at a dinner table

— and marriage to Dr. Fernandez! And you can take it from me that that is one thing she intends to bring off one day!"

Lisa said nothing to this.

"However, all that's beside the point, except that at the moment Doña Beatriz is suffering slightly from frustration, and feeling frustrated she's inclined to be spiteful. She doesn't want to make things too easy for you, and she could make things awkward. I'd rather get you away from the house sometimes; take you to the cinema in San Cecilio, take you out to dinner — things like that. No watching eyes, no comments. And there's another thing. I've an aunt who's coming to visit me soon, or to look me up, at least. She's my aunt Grizel, short for Grizelda, and nobody knows how old she is, because she looks as if she might go on living for ever! She has a flat in Madrid, and her great hobby is painting. She has painted her way right round the world, or so she boasts, and every now and again she has exhibitions of her pictures in places like London and Paris I suppose she's really quite an artist. However, the main thing is she wants to come and see me in my cottage, and I'll have to give her lunch. I'll take her to an hotel, of course, and I'd like you to join us. I think you'd enjoy meeting her, because she's quite unlike the usual run of aunts, and fairly bright and breezy. Will you do so, Lisa?"

Lisa didn't hesitate over this.

"Oh, yes, I'd like to," she said. And, she thought, Spanish sensibilities couldn't possibly be upset by her meeting with the aunt of an attractive young man like Peter Hamilton-Tracey, and joining the two of them for a meal. And although she was quite well aware that Dr. Fernandez didn't approve of her association with Peter for the simple reason that it could prove unsettling to her daily life, and affect the quality of the service he demanded as an employer — there couldn't possibly be any other reason why he should object! — she agreed with Peter that the atmosphere of the villa since the arrival of Doña Beatriz was not quite the light-hearted atmosphere it had been before she left Madrid.

Sometimes even the thought of Doña Beatriz weighed upon her, like a cloud she could do nothing to lift, because by comparison with herself she was all things elegant and sophisticated, and her relationship with Dr. Fernandez was so very different from the relationship of a girl who was filling a temporary post, and not yet entirely trusted.

And one day, of course, she would marry Dr. Fernandez. . . . When he had recognized how futile it was to continue dwelling upon the past, and the brief happiness that had once been his, and realized how much she had to offer him!

It was only a question of time. Peter was right about that.

When Peter said goodnight and went back to his cottage he carried with him her reiterated promise to meet his aunt, and he in his turn promised to let her know in good time when that aunt threatened to arrive. Then she could approach her employer for permission to absent herself for the first whole day that had been granted to her since he became her employer.

CHAPTER NINE

BUT BEFORE that day dawned an incident happened that caused her to see him in quite a different light from any that she had so far seen him in.

Señora Cortina was in the habit of receiving vegetables at the side entrance to the villa, and these were brought to her daily by the young man who drove a donkey-cart down a narrow lane that was an offshoot of the winding main road, and brought the cart to rest outside a creaking iron gate. The creaking of the gate usually announced his arrival, and Señora Cortina would emerge in her apron — frequently wiping her hands on it as if she had only just deserted the kitchen sink — and scold him in a loud voice for being late with cauliflowers, or the crisp hearts of lettuce that she was to arrange into a salad for lunch.

This was so much part of a daily ritual that Lisa and her charge often listened for it at about the hour when they knew that that shrill and rebuking voice would shatter the drowsy silence of the garden, Following the grating of wheels on the rough surface of the lane, the creaking of the gate, and then leisured footsteps making their way to the side door, they would cease whatever they were doing, lift up their heads, and then smile at one another when the tirade broke out.

"This is a fine hour of the day in which to bring vegetables for lunch! . . . *For lunch!*" The voice would reach a pitch of indignation. "It is the laziness in your bones that you are suffering from, Pedro Gonzalez, and the sooner you do something to overcome it the better for us all! The better for my cooking! . . ."

Then would follow wheedling compliments in a sleepy male voice on the undoubted quality of that cooking, and more often than not the offender — in spite of the lateness of the hour — would be invited inside for some refreshment which he had scarcely earned. And when he emerged, after the lapse of a quarter of an hour or so, at least, and he caught sight of Gia peeping through a gap in the hedge, with Lisa standing more properly a little way from her, he would wink at them both with one of his handsome black Spanish eyes, and then climb back on to his cart and grind leisurely away.

Spain is the country of *mañana* — tomorrow! — and with Pedro Gonzalez tomorrow could just as well be the day after tomorrow, judging by the perpetual sleepiness of his expression, and the deliberate care with which he avoided any sign of anything approaching haste. He was, Lisa supposed, typical of a good many young men in that part of the world, a Catalan, indolent by nature, with little purpose in the beyond the day-to-day routine, and the occasional bullfight and *fiesta*. She would imagine his lassitude slipping from him a little at *fiesta* time, or when he was encouraging a favorite matador in the bull-ring, and his black eyes could certainly work overtime if a pretty girl was anywhere in his vicinity.

Lisa he had eyed casually at first, and then with increasing interest when he saw her on several occasions. Gia described him, giggling at her own descripton, as "Pedro the vegetable man who liked the look of Lisa!" But Lisa saw nothing either apt or funny in this, and apart from smiling at Señora Cortina's outbursts when he arrived with the vegetables, she preferred to keep out of the orbit of his black glance if possible when he was in the vicinity.

She wasn't used to men of his type — down-to-earth, sensual types, with a look of brutality at the corners of a handsome mouth—and she shrank from being silently approved of. Also, for some reason, she had an active mistrust of Pedro, and this wasn't anything at all to do with the looks he directed at himself.

One morning he arrived at the side gate with a huge black mongrel dog sitting up beside him in the cart. The dog wasn't merely a mongrel of the worst vintage — and there were many mongrels whom Lisa had fallen in love with on sight! — but he was shamefully neglected, and he looked bad-tempered. He was sitting on a sack of onions when the cart drew up, and he lifted his lip and showed his teeth in an ominous manner when Pedro thrust him aside in order to lift the sack on his back and deposit it inside Señora Cortina's kitchen, and a low growl left his throat. Pedro gave him a hearty slap that sent him into a corner of the cart, and when he looked round and saw Lisa attempting to persuade Gia away from the hole in the hedge he treated her to a display of his hard white teeth.

"You like dogs, *señorita*?" he asked, in his languid manner. "All English people like dogs, and make the great fuss of them! Is that not so? *Si?*"

Lisa did not reply, and he settled the sack of onions more comfortably on his back, gave the dog a second thrust away from a box of lettuces, and then with his eyes still on her continued conversationally:

"This fellow not good-tempered fellow. Very bad-tempered dog. Yesterday he fight and kill another much smaller than himself, and I give him a whipping. Today he not forget, and growl at me. Tonight I give him another whipping!"

"Then it's no wonder that he's bad-tempered!" Lisa could not prevent herself from saying in a burst of indignation.

"You think so?" He leaned against the cart, the sack of onions dangling like an indolent cloak from his broad back, and his black eyes blazed with a mixture of amusement and mockery. "Ah, but that is because you are English, and in England it is the habit to fuss the dog! The little pet dog! *Si?*"

"That is no pet dog," Lisa told him, eyeing the mongrel apprehensively, for Gia was making overtures to it, and they were not being well received. She drew Gia back from the gap in the hedge, and, while Pedro thought up more provocative things to say, became aware out of the tail of her eye of Señora Cortina's recently acquired puppy (also of doubtful ancestry) emerging ahead of its owner from the partly opened side door and preparing to take a stroll along the path. Señora Cortina hadn't yet heard the iron gate creak, and the puppy was temporarily free and obviously filled with a sense of adventure, and its small paws padded happily along the path until it heard the growl of the older dog. Only when it heard that growl and paused, its long spaniel-like ears twitching alertly, its terrier eyes displaying sudden uncertainty, did Lisa realize that something had got to be done about it —and done quickly!

Most well-trained dogs respect the inexperience of a puppy — even when its appearance is distinctly odd, as in the case of Señora Cortina's pet, which had been acquired because her husband had taken a fancy to it, and she did occasionally give way to her husband. But not so Pedro's big, ugly-looking black dog, who followed up his first growl with a violent, annoyed bark, and then leapt through the air and landed upon the puppy.

But not before Lisa had anticipated the leap, and herself moved like an uncoiled spring in order to secure the safety of the puppy. As she snatched it up — and it felt like a bundle of soft bones in her hand, covered by extra-ordinarily silky skin—Gia let out a shriek of warning, which was, however, much too late. For the black dog landed upon Lisa instead of the puppy, and it bore her to the ground with ease, since its proportions were massive and it was full of a kind of frenzy. Without being clearly aware how she had even forced her way through that gap in the hedge to reach the path, Lisa found herself sprawled at full length on the ground, with the cause of the trouble now seriously threatening her as well as the tiny creature she sought to preserve.

Gia shrieked again, and then called upon Pedro to do something. But his movements were leisurely as he moved to the assistance of the English girl, and it was only something he said softly in Spanish that caused the dog to become immobile as if by magic, while still displaying its ugly yellow teeth.

Pedro put out a hand and helped a dazed Lisa to her feet, and he addressed her in the same soft tone.

"Next time it will be as well if you do not interfere, *señorita*."

· But he got no farther, for a furious voice behind him ordered him to get outside with his sack of onions, *and* his dog, and stay outside; and Gia flew to her father's side and caught at his arm and held it tightly while she explained exactly what had happened, and how brave Lisa had been.

"It was the puppy, Papa! She thought the big dog would do it some harm — that it would be killed!"

"It might very easily have done you some harm, Miss Waring!" Julio Fernandez said, with a tight, enclosed look about his face, and utterly inscrutable eyes, as Lisa stood awkwardly hugging the puppy and looking up at him in a bewildered way. As she thrust back a long end of her hair that had fallen across her forehead and he caught sight of the ugly graze on her arm his expression tightened still more, and his voice was short and clipped as he demanded: "Are you quite sure that brute didn't touch you? That mark on your arm——"

"Just contact with the gravel of the path, I think," she answered, looking at it ruefully, and then attempting to smile lightly. "Yes; that's all it is. No worse damage! And the puppy's quite safe — trembling all over, but otherwise quite all right!" She gave the little animal an affectionate look, and then as the strand of golden hair fell forward again put it back with slim fingers that were shaking noticeably. Inside herself she was also feeling a little sick, for the whole affair had happened very suddenly, and she had no clear warning that it was going to happen until it was practically over. She still felt bewildered; her own movements had been purely instinctive, and she had no idea how she had thrust her way through the gap in the hedge in the very nick of time to be of service to the puppy.

But the important thing was that she *had* been of service to the puppy.

"I don't think Pedro's dog likes puppies," she said, rather foolishly, and then felt a powerfully persuasive arm about her shoulders, and knew that she was directed towards the house.

As the pleasant dimness of the interior of the villa closed round them Señora Cortina's voice could be heard scolding the vegetable man unmercifully, and he was protesting as his onions were once more stowed away in his cart. Lisa thought it a little hard that, as the result of the intrepidity of the puppy, he should lose a valuable customer, and as a brandy glass was placed in her hand, after she herself had been installed in a

99

comfortable leather chair in the library, she heard herself making feeble excuses for him.

"It wasn't really Pedro's fault. His dog is untrained and naturally unpredictable, I'd say. But it did obey him when he called it off. I don't know what he said, but it did obey him. And, in any case, I don't suppose it would have touched me."

"Drink up that brandy," the doctor ordered quietly, and when she had done so took the glass away from her. He stood looking down at her. "In this country it is not wise to interfere in animal disputes. Our people are not trained to regard them as your people at home. You must remember that in future."

"I will," she promised, and an embarrassed color struggled into her cheeks as his grave dark eyes studied her. He was Spanish in such a dignified, attractive way, she thought, almost wistfully — not flamboyantly Spanish, like Pedro! Even had he been born into a similar station in life, doomed to concentrate on vegetables as his main means of sustenance, and to hawk them from door to door, he would still be completely unlike Pedro. Humane, and emotionally stable — emotionally economical! — with a wisdom at the back of those night-dark eyes that was like the wisdom of the ages, because he obviously saw so much, and thought so much more than one might suspect him of at a first meeting.

As in a flash she recalled her own first meeting with him — not the first time she saw him, but the first time she actually came face to face with him on the little jetty in San Cecilio, with the moon shedding its light over the sea. He had been charming and kind. Later she had discovered that he could be hard and cold. Just now she wasn't at all certain what was going on behind the emotionless mask of his face, but once more he was being kind.

All at once a sensation of desolation swept over her. He was kind to her because she had been foolhardy, and a big black mongrel dog had knocked her down, and her arm had been grazed. He had already examined the graze very carefully, and now he asked her to excuse him for a moment while he withdrew to some corner of the house where he kept the materials for cleansing it, and ensuring that it became nothing worse than a graze.

When he returned she was wallowing in the trough of her desolation, and the brandy he had persuaded her to drink had in some way acted as a depressant, which she knew it shouldn't have done. Unless it was that she had been secretly very much depressed beforehand — in fact, for several days — and the brandy was the key that opened the door to all her carefully controlled emotions. Whatever it was, however, she was in no mood just then to analyze her feelings, and she only knew that they seemed to be getting the better of her, particularly when he knelt beside her, and his sleek dark head came very close to the tip of her chin. And the sudden smarting of the graze when he treated it with something out of a bottle brought a rush of tears to her eyes, and she gave a little gasp, and one of them splashed down on to the back of his hand.

He looked up as if he was startled.

"That hurt you!" he exclaimed. "I'm sorry, but it is important that this sort of thing should not be neglected——"

And then he saw how she bit at her trembling lower lip, as waves of mortification rushed up over her.

"It's nothing!" she assured him, managing to get the words out somehow. "I'm not normally a coward, only——"

"Only this morning is rather different, because you have had a shock, and also you were very much concerned because the well-being of that extraordinary-looking creature Señora Cortina calls a puppy was most unexpectedly threatened!" he said, and his voice was infinitely gentle. "I know! I understand!"

She looked up at him helplessly, and the tears were still swimming in her eyes, so that they looked like grey-blue violets drenched with dew; and despite every effort on her part her traitorous lower lip would not be steady.

If only he did understand, she thought! If only he understood just what his nearness did to her, and how completely barren her whole future stretched before her because of it! And then panic seized her lest she should give herself away. and he should be horrified, and dismiss her — send her back to England. . . .

"Please do forgive me," she begged, in a terror-stricken little rush. "It was the iodine, I think. . . . I wasn't prepared for it."

But his whole expression had undergone a complete change, and the lustrous dark eyes were suddenly full of concern. He rose from his kneeling position and took a chair beside her, leaning forward and possessing himself of both her hands, and holding them strongly.

"*Querida*," he said — and she was certain the endearment escaped him by accident — "something rather more than that is wrong, I think? You are not hurt anywhere else, are you? That brute of a dog didn't——"

"No, no," she assured him, sounding calm as his agitation mounted.

"Then your fall was rather worse than I was able to observe? I was a little late on the scene, otherwise there would have been no fall of any kind! You are badly shaken — bruised?"

She smiled determinedly through her tears, and then successfully willed them away.

"I am perfectly all right," she assured him.

He looked down at her hands, and the sight of them lying in his virile brown palms seemed to fascinate him. They were so slender and white and well cared for, and not for the first time they struck him as very fragile hands, and inadequate for one who had to earn her own living.

"Nevertheless I think you ought to go upstairs to your room and lie down. Perhaps I ought to give you a sedative. . . ."

She gently removed her hands.

"Nonsense, Doctor. I shall be completely myself once I've had an opportunity to change my dress" — looking down at the rent in the pink linen caused by a branch that had clutched at her during her fall — "and washed and tidied myself." She was conscious that there was dust on her cheek, and her hair would persist in falling forward so that it was more like a golden cloak framing her face.

Slowly the doctor's eyes lifted from her hands to her face, and although there was no longer any sign of weakness, and she was completely in control of all her emotions, the troubled look in his eyes persisted. Also he seemed to find her face, unrevealing though it now was, as temporarily fascinating as her hands.

"*Que* — Miss Waring," he said, so swiftly that there might never have been any hesitation over his choice of a manner of addressing her, "will you tell me whether you are really happy here!"

She looked at him in surprise.

"Happy? But of course I'm happy."

"And you do not regret that you ever came to Spain?"

Her eyes widened, and her pulses quickened because she was suddenly once more afraid. He had guessed. . . . He was guessing!

"I love Spain!"

His eyes were still troubled, and his voice was troubled, too.

"We once talked of roses, you and I — and the one perfect one to be found one day in a garden. For you, that is. . . ." His eyes held hers for a moment, and then he looked away. He stood up, and moved away to the window. "Your young friend, Peter Hamilton-Tracey, telephoned me this morning and asked for permission to take you out to lunch with a relative of his. Some elderly aunt who has arrived to stay in San Cecilio, and whom he wishes you to meet. Presumably he also wishes her to meet you. . . ."

He turned and looked at her fixedly.

"Yes," she answered, as casually as she could, "I was expecting the invitation."

"And you were also expecting to meet the aunt?"

"Yes, I—I was told about her."

His eyes held a look she simply could not understand.

"When young men introduce young women friends to their relatives they are usually rather serious about them." He started to pace up and down the library. "At least, in Spain it would indicate rather more than seriousness! I have no very clear idea how you conduct these things in your country, but I feel in a sense responsible for you, and my advice to you is, do not let lonliness drive you into a situation that you might find it difficult to extricate yourself from. That is," with a queer smile just touching the corners of his lips, "if you still feel the same way about roses!"

"I——" Lisa was beginning, when the door opened and Doña Beatriz stood looking with distinct curiosity at both of them.

"I heard that you were here," she said, "and that Miss Waring had been foolish enough to interfere with a mongrel dog!" Her voice suggested that, having done such a thing, Miss Waring had received her deserts. "Señora Cortina is in a state of despair in the kitchen, because her vegetable supply is low, and the vegetable man has gone on his way without leaving her any onions or leeks for the soup. So next time, Miss Waring," with a cold smile, "that you think to save her puppy's life for her, remember also that she has an employer whom she is paid to serve, and that the proper preparation of his meals is of the utmost importance!"

Lisa stood up. She could hardly believe that Señora Cortina had been so ungrateful that she actually complained about her — or even about the shortage of vegetables for lunch! — but she had seen the way in which Doña Beatriz's eyes had darted between the two of them, her employer and herself, and that it had not passed her by that at the moment of her entry they had not been discussing either puppies, or the damage Lisa had caused herself as a result of her affection for one of them.

In fact, Doña Beatriz suddenly looked a little grim, especially when she caught sight of the empty brandy glass on the table, and the various medicaments that had been used in the treatment of Lisa's arm.

"So much trouble," she said curtly, and for such a little thing!"

"It was not a little thing to Miss Waring." Dr. Fernandez replied, almost as curtly. And then, to Lisa: "I think it would be as well if you remained in your room until dinner-time tonight, Miss Waring. I will see that a tray of lunch is sent to you, and I recommend that you undress and go to bed. Tonight, if you are fit, we shall be delighted to see you at dinner."

Lisa could almost feel Doña Beatriz's surprise as she went out of the room, and she knew that the

Spanish woman would never forgive the slight snub in front of her. But she would vent her displeasure on her, Lisa — not Julio Fernandez!

As she closed the door she heard Doña Beatriz say, more soothingly:

"Poor Julio! How these things always recoil on you! But I don't suppose the girl was really hurt, was she?"

"She might have been badly mauled."

"It was a stupid thing to do. And for a bundle of bones that ought not to be given house-room! But, then, you are too kind to your servants, as well as that girl. For the remainder of today I suppose she will consider herself an invalid, and who will look after Gia? She really ought to remember that Gia is her main preoccupation."

Lisa did not hear the conclusion of this conversation, but she recognized that Doña Beatriz was right in what she said. Gia *was* her main preoccupation, and while she received such a handsome salary for looking after her she ought to concentrate on looking after her and nothing else.

Nothing else! . . . She walked to her dressing-table mirror when she reached her own room, and the sight of her dishevelled appearance appalled her, especially when she recalled that Dr. Fernandez had gazed at it quite earnestly — as if he derived a certain amount of rather curious pleasure from doing so!

She picked up a comb and automatically ran it through her hair, having no intention whatsoever of shirking her duties for the rest of that day and retiring to bed. And her pulses quickened as she recalled the doctor's words:

". . . *If you still feel the same way about roses!*"

The one perfect rose in the garden! But it was hardly likely it would ever be for her.

CHAPTER TEN

THE LUNCH for Peter's Aunt Grizelda was a great success, and after it was over Lisa was able to admit to herself that she had enjoyed every moment of it.

Aunt Grizel, for one thing, was quite unlike anyone she had ever met before, and if ever a personality had a stimulating quality about her, she had it. She was Miss Grizel Tracey, possibly somewhere in her early sixties, with close-cropped hair, shaggy white eyebrows that overhung a lively and humorous — and shrewd — pair of greyish-blue eyes, and a weather-beaten face that had remained throughout its life as Nature intended it. No light dusts of powder for Miss Tracey, skin tonics or creams to disguise the fine networks of wrinkles that had probably formed soon after she was thirty at the corners of her eyes and mouth, largely because she had a habit of throwing back her head and laughing until the eyes nearly closed, and her lips were so frequently stretched above her excellent dentures that the skin had become loosened at the corners, and lost most of its elasticity. But that would never bother Aunt Grizel. Any more than prematurely white hair had bothered her, and it would certainly never occur to her to use a colorful rinse that would make it look absolutely lovely.

Aunt Grizel had made up her mind in her teens that she was not good-looking, and that marriage would probably pass her by. And the fact that it had passed her by had not embittered her.

She could chat happily about her old school friends' domestic problems now that they were grandmothers, and chuckle wickedly because they were never likely to overtake her. Such problems as daughters who expected rather a lot in the way of baby-sitting, and older grand-children for whom some sort of a permanent home had to be maintained in order that they could spend at least a part of their holidays with their grandmother.

"The only grandchildren I've got are the pic-tures I've never sold," she admitted, "and those I cart happily about the world with me because I can't bear to be without them. And as I couldn't bear a permanent home they're the ideal grand-children for me."

Although it was a very warm day, with the temperature likely to rise a good deal higher during the afternoon, she wore a tweed suit and nylon stockings of heavy mesh, and the only vice she apeared to have cultivated — that of smok-ing heavily, even between the courses of a meal — provided Lisa with a real surprise when, dur-ing the coffee stage of the lunch, she tried to induce her nephew to accept one of the long, dark, Spanish cigarettes she extracted from a pocket of her handbag.

She caught Lisa's eyes, with surprise written largely in them, fixed on her, and her own eyes twinkled as she explained:

"I love Spanish cigarettes, just as I love every-thing Spanish — the food, the wines, the people, the scenery, the *fiestas*, the bullfights! Yes: even bullfights!" Her eyes twinkled still more as Lisa strove politely to conceal her surprise. "They're not half as gory as they're made out to be, you know — when you get over the initial shock, and the excitement begins to get hold of you. Have you ever shared in the excitement of a real Spanish crowd?" she asked the girl. "Felt it make your blood flow more quickly, as if you'd had too much champagne?"

Lisa shook her head. Then she explained, with a faintly humorous smile of her own:

"But I've never had too much champagne, either."

Aunt Grizel sent her a quizzical glance.

"Then that's an experience in store for you — a pleasant experience so long as it is only a *little* too much!" Her eyes seemed to find the girl an interesting study, and the fact that her nephew had been so keen for them to meet had intrigued her before ever the meeting had taken place. "My nephew tells me you came to Spain for a holiday. Miss Waring, and remained to look after some child or other. That looking after children is your job. Do you enjoy it?"

"Oh, yes," Lisa assured her, and as she looked around the cool, airy, principal lounge of San Cecilio's leading hotel — the hotel where she had passed that fortnight of her holiday — she could have added that it was here that she had met the man who was the father of the child since become her charge. But for some reason she didn't do so. Miss Tracey's eyes were very shrewd — a little too shrewd, perhaps — and Lisa was afraid she might give herself away if she spoke of Dr. Fernandez. She might color, or her eyes might reveal something. . . . So she left it to Peter to explain casually:

"By the way, Aunt Grizel, you probably know Lisa's employer. Fellow called Fernandez. Dr. Julio Fernandez. Practices in Madrid, and looks as if he ought to be terribly well-known. Heart specialist, or something. . . ."

"Julio Fernandez?" Aunt Grizel looked interested. "Oh, yes, I know him. Or I know of him." She explained to Lisa: "I have a flat in Madrid, and although I only stay there for a part of each year, I do know quite a lot of people whom I meet frequently when I'm in the capital. Spaniards love entertaining, and they do it very well, and as it happens your Dr. Fernandez is socially very much sought after. He's a widower, isn't he? And he isn't a heart specialist, Peter, he's a neurologist."

"Well, hearts and minds go together, don't they? Peter murmured flippantly. "The one is never affected, in an emotional sense, unless the other sanctions the interference with normal routine," looking at Lisa with an oblique, amused blue gaze.

Aunt Grizel shook her head at him.

"Dr. Fernandez is not interested in the mental attitude that is the result of some wayward capitulation of the heart. Although, as a matter of fact"— looking as if she was not above a bit of gossip when it came her way — "there *is* a rather devastating widow who has been doing her best to trap him into a second incursion into matrimony for several years now, and his friends will have it that she'll succeed one day. The marvel is that she hasn't succeeded before this, because she's quite ravishing in the way some of these Spanish women are, and a doctor needs a wife — particularly a doctor of his eminence. Socially she's practically indispensible, and it must have been a bit of a handicap to him to struggle along without one for so long."

"I think you're referring to our Doña Beatriz," Peter said, "when you speak of a ravishing Spanish widow, and I agree with the doctor's friends that he won't have to struggle along with a handicap much longer." Again he looked at Lisa, but questioningly this time. "Don't you agree with me, Lisa? Aren't all the signs at the moment indicating that your employer will provide his motherless child with a substitute mother before very long?"

"I——" Lisa knew that anyone with any powers of observation would agree with him, but somehow she couldn't, and she felt rather than saw Miss Tracey's eyes become attracted to her as if she was a magnet.

"You — what, Miss Waring?" the older woman asked, with a bright sparkle of alertness in her eyes. She put her close-cropped white head on one side, and looked at the girl from that angle. "If you're looking after Dr. Fernandez' child you probably know a litle more about him than we do. Is it true that he's packing the child off to school in England this autumn?"

"There is talk of it," Lisa admitted. "I think," she added, "Doña Beatriz, who is the doctor's guest at the moment, is rather keen for him to do so."

"Ah!" Aunt Grizel exclaimed, as if that explained a great deal. "Then she'll probably win, for I believe the child — whom I've never met — is a plain little monkey, quite unlike her beautiful mother, whose death, everyone says, upset the doctor so very much that he never took kindly to his only child. Which always strikes me as a most unnatural attitude on the part of a father."

"Not if — if her birth caused the death of the woman he loved," Lisa felt forced to defend her employer, but the words sounded stiff and unnatural as they left her lips.

Miss Tracey loked at her as if she was really beginning to interest her.

"Tell me," she asked suddenly, "how much you like your job? You find that you fit into a Spanish household?"

Lisa hesitated, not because she was uncertain, but because she felt embarrassed.

"I like it very much," she admitted at last. "But it will only last until the autumn —or until Dr. Fernandez makes up his mind about his daughter's future."

"Or Doña Beatriz makes it up for him?"

"Perhaps."

"And after that you will go home? Back to England?" Lisa nodded.

"You won't look for another job in Spain?"

"I — don't think so."

This time it was Aunt Grizel who nodded, as if she understood perfectly, and then she changed the subject by asking her nephew about his cottage, and insisting that they went there for tea.

It was the first time Lisa had actually visited Peter's cottage, although she had seen the outside of it when she and Gia had been sauntering along the white road from which it lay back in a grove of trees. It was a typical small, white-washed, Spanish cottage, with a green-tiled roof, and shutters that were fastened back against the walls. The garden was unkempt because nobody ever worked in it, but inside a local Catalan employ maintained a certain amount of order, and if the furnishings were bare and crude, they didn't shock his aunt.

"You could do worse," she said. "I rented a place like this myself once, on this very same coast, and did some wonderful work, because the light is so extraordinarily perfect, and there were so many subjects for my canvases." She looked in the kitchen for tea, and when she discovered that there was none produced a packet from her capacious handbag of stout crocodile skin. "I brought this for you," she said, "because I expected you'd be living on coffee, and I have some sent out from England regularly. The one thing I can't do without is my cup of tea!"

Lisa rather enjoyed that alfresco meal, with Peter apologizing for the discomforts and the deficiencies, and looking embarrassed when it was discovered that he actually did some of his own washing, because the woman he employed wasn't very good at it, and she was even worse at ironing.

"In fact, she's not a very good cook, either," Peter had to admit. "Some of the meals she serves up are practically inedible, and run largely to greasy stews and lashings of garlic, so I eat out mostly. But fortunately I don't have to pay rent for this place, so my currency is being eked out quite comfortably."

"And what happens when it has run out altogether?" his aunt inquired, sitting on a backless chair in the kitchen and drinking with relish the strong tea she had brewed.

Peter looked vague.

"I don't quite know." In addition to the fact that he had been ill recently, he appeared to have the kind of temperament that refused to allow him to settle down in one particular job, and the fact that he had a certain amount of talent as a writer was another reason why the very thought of a routine job was inclined to upset him. He looked at Lisa. "I'm like Lisa here — I drift from one rather uncongenial job to another, and hope that in the next I will find the answer to all my secret dreams and aspirations!"

His aunt made a disapproving noise.

"Then the sooner you make up your mind about your secret dreams and aspirations the better, unless you want to turn into a Mr. Micawber, continually hoping that something will 'turn up'! But I decline to believe that Lisa" — by this time she had abandoned the more formal Miss Waring — "is looking for anything very special from her jobs, apart from the one thing most young women look for. And as an old maid I can voice it as my opinion that it is a good thing to look for, if you don't want to be lonely all your days — and of course I'm talking about marriage!" She focused her gaze carefully on the girl, to witness her reactions. "Marriage is for young women like Lisa — and she knows it! Don't you, my dear?"

Lisa blushed almost painfully, and borrowed a teaspoon to remove a tea-leaf from her cup.

"I suppose there are other things," she murmured, rather inaudibly.

Miss Tracey shook her head.

"Not for girls who look like you! I never had golden hair, and a skin like a drift of apple blossom (quite a relief after the sallow complexions one sees around here, even to an old woman like me, so I wonder at the effect on some of the younger Spaniards with whom you must already have come in contact!) and eyes——" She seemed to run out of descriptive adjectives when she got to Lisa's eyes, so she suddenly sighed and shook her head. "So I got passed over, and remained single, and although it never bothered me at all I wouldn't recommend it for Lisa!"

All at once she seemed to have an idea.

"You must come and stay with me in Madrid when your job comes to an end, my dear. I've only a tiny flat, but there's room enough for you, if you don't mind sharing what space there is with a lot of artist's clutter! And I'll show you Madrid, and believe me there's a lot to see there — and provide you with some pleasanter memories to carry back to England than the inside of a Spanish nursery. And if Peter is still trying to make up his mind about his future he can come to. I can't put him up, but we'll find him a reasonable guest-house, and I don't mind footing the bill," looking at her nephew, "if it will enable you to make up your mind what you *do* want to do with your life, apart from waste it!"

He smiled ruefully.

"I shouldn't think there's anything I can do in Spain."

"Not anything you can do in Spain, perhaps — but you can always arrive at a few conclusions, and they might enable you to make a few decisions," with so much meaning in her look that he appeared suddenly enlightened, and grinned.

"I see," he said. "I see!"

"I wonder whether you do," she remarked obscurely, and started to gather up the cups and saucers. 'We'll wash these up for you before I go back to my hotel, and Lisa returns to her charge. And remember, Lisa, I shall look forward to seeing you in the autumn — and before that, if you can get away. Perhaps you could get away for a few days' break? Madrid is bracing in the cooler weather, but the color and the magic are there in the height of summer."

Lisa thanked her, but she didn't think it likely that she would get a few days' break — and she knew that she would shrink from asking for them. Doña Beatriz would almost certainly elevate her eyebrows and look amazed when the information was passed on to her that the English girl failed to look upon her well-paid holiday post *as* a holiday post — which of course it was!

Gia was not actually receiving much tuition, and their days were passed in a pleasant monotony of sunshine and aimless attempts to amuse themselves against a background of blue sea and brilliant color. Therefore, what more could the English girl want — or expect?

At least, that was what Lisa imagined would be Doña Beatriz's reaction if she asked for a few days to go and stay with Grizelda Tracey in Madrid.

Her surprise, therefore, was considerable when she returned to the villa to find that her employer wished to see her in his library immediately she was available; and as a result of that visit to the library Madrid became a solution to a slightly awkward problem.

Dr. Fernandez was standing thoughtfully before the long window that opened outwards into the patio when she received permission to enter, following her light tap at the door. It was such a light tap, and the door was so beautifully solid,

115

that he scarcely heard it, as a matter of fact, but he had been waiting for it, and he turned immediately she entered.

"Sit down, Miss Waring." He pushed a chair towards her. "I hope you have enjoyed your outing with your friends?"

"Oh, yes."

"The lunch went off very well?"

"Very well," she echoed mechanically. He was wearing a light grey suit, irreproachably cut, as were all his clothes, and his linen was almost startlingly white, and his narrow black silk tie made him look somehow very Spanish. Or that was the impression she received of him, with the shadows of the library emphasizing the blackness and the thickness of his hair, and his olive skin a little more noticeably olive than usual. And his manner struck her as very formal — which, of course, was very Spanish.

"You made the acquaintance of Mr. Hamilton-Tracey's aunt?"

"Miss Tracey? Oh, yes. I liked her very much."

"Good!" He moved away and touched some papers on his desk. "And I have no doubt she also liked you very much?"

"I'm afraid I can't answer that one." She tried to laugh lightly, naturally, as if he was merely being humorous, instead of so painfully stiff and dignified. "But we got on quite well together, I think, and she expressed a desire to see me again."

"Then that is excellent, and your Peter Hamilton-Tracey must be very well satisfied."

Her slim eyebrows drew together.

"There's no real reason why he should be feeling very satisfied, except that I helped him to entertain his aunt."

"No?" He picked up a gold-mounted fountain-pen, and tapped it on the back of his nails. "Miss Waring, it pleases me that you have had a pleasant

116

break from the daily routine, but now I have something to say to you. You will have a somewhat longer break from routine — a week, or possibly even a fortnight — because Doña Beatriz wishes to take Gia back with her to Madrid. There are various important items, such as a dental overhaul, and the acquisition of some new clothes, which Doña Beatriz considers must be attended to at once, if Gia is to be ready for school in the autumn."

"I see." But Lisa's eyes had opened wide with something like amazement, and she sat up very straight in her chair. "But, if Gia is to get to school in the autumn, surely it will be necessary first to decide upon the school she is to attend, and the kind of uniform she will have to wear? And until you have done that——"

He shrugged in a way that struck her as impatient.

"Whether or not she goes to school in the autumn, clothes are something she must have. Doña Beatriz has been going through her wardrobe, and apparently it is rather badly deficient."

"I would have said that, for a small girl, it's anything but deficient," Lisa heard herself saying with a decisiveness she had never used to him before.

He turned and looked at her, noticeably frowning.

"And you know a lot about small girls and their requirements — is that it, Miss Waring? More than Beatriz, for instance?"

She bit her lip.

"I know when they have all, and more, than they want. And from a purely material point of view I would say that Gia has everything she wants."

"From a material point of view — only?"

"I didn't say that!"

"No, you didn't say it," with a tightening of his lips, "and as an employee I think you would be wise if you didn't even think it!" He moved away from her again and stood staring stonily out of the window. "My daughter, Miss Waring, has received every possible attention from the moment she was born, and as her father I will see to it that she continues to receive every possible attention! She has also received an extraordinary amount of kindness from Doña Beatriz!"

"I'm sure of it," Lisa said, feeling herself much more than merly rebuked, while the color on her cheek-bones felt as if it was burning holes in them. "I was only venturing an opinion that, at the moment, she has a very well stocked wardrobe."

"That is for Doña Beatriz to decide!"

"Of course."

But although her voice was quiet, and almost demure, inside her something was quaking with an uprush of nothing short of anger. Why was it any more Doña Beatriz's concern than it was hers? Doña Beatriz was merely an invited guest in his house — not, so far as she was aware, his fiancée, and certainly not his wife. Not yet, at any rate. And Lisa had been employed to take full charge of Gia!

"Then am I to understand that Doña Beatriz will have Gia to stay with her in Madrid?" she asked in the same governess-like tone.

"That is the plan," with a motionless back.

"She will not be — be staying with you?"

Hardly — if she is to stay with Doña Beatriz!"

"And what do you want me to do?"

He turned in surprise.

"Why, remain here, of course! Have you any objections to a short holiday from your pupil?"

"None whatsoever, only — it has occurred to me that Doña Beatriz has never really approved of me as a close companion for Gia, and as you obviously value her opinion you might think this a good opportunity to terminate the arrangement altogether!" Her voice and face were perfectly composed, the demure look very deceptive, and the surprise in his eyes grew until she could have sworn, for one instant, there was an ingredient of concern mixed up with it. "I shall quite understand if you would like me to look upon this as dismissal, Dr. Fernandez. And from every point of view it might be as well if you employed someone to take charge of Gia, until she does go to school, whom Doña Beatriz can approve!"

She thought he sent her a long, and distinctly curious, look; but his voice was quiet and emotionless as he asked:

"And you, Miss Waring? Once again you are referring to points of view—this time 'every point of view'! Does that mean you would accept dismissal with equanimity?"

She lifted her slender shoulders slightly — a gesture she might have copied from Señora Cortina, who was doing it continually.

"I think, yes, I could accept it with equanimity. You see, I never really expected that this position with your daughter would last long."

"Why not?"

"Oh, I don't know. . . ." This time it was she who half turned away. "Perhaps I was never certain that I could give satisfaction, and you took me on without really knowing anything at all about me."

The doctor ignored this.

"You are fond of Gia?" he wanted to know.

"Oh, yes — very fond!" Suddenly her face softened. "Terribly fond!" she heard herself adding, because it was no more than the truth.

"And she, I have reason to believe, is very fond of you, therefore that disposes of any failure on your part to give satisfaction."

"But there is still Doña Beatriz." She deliberately avoided meeting his eyes, that were so dark and lustrous and probing. "I think it's quite natural that she should consider a Spanish girl — or possibly even some other nationality — would be better suited to Gia than I, in her opinion, will ever be."

"But it is I," he reminded her, "who employs you!"

She looked at him — just for a moment she peeped at him — and her eyes asked the question, "Do you?", while her lips made use of words that had a meek quiescence about them.

"Of course," she said.

All at once it was impossible to doubt that he was annoyed, and his annoyance caused his black brows to meet above the bridge of his straight nose, and the eyes below them sparkled frostily. His lips tightened, his square chin seemed suddenly to become very noticeable, and his voice was crisp when he said:

"Then, unless you have some very strong reason of your own for wishing, as you put it, to terminate our arrangement — an arrangement arrived at when I did know little or nothing about you!" he reminded her, and she wondered dully whether he thought he knew very much more about her now — "perhaps you will be good enough to remain with Gia at least until the summer is over, and some other more permanent plans have been made for her. Will you do that, Miss Waring? Or do you seriously wish to be replaced?"

"No — no, I don't,"she admitted, and some compulsion in his regard forced her to meet it for longer than a bare half second or so, and while the grey eyes and the black eyes met she was in imminent danger of adding to the admission— of yielding to a wild impulse and crying out to him. "Of course I don't want to go away! . . . I couldn't *bear* to go away! It will be bad enough when you return to Madrid, but please don't send me right away out of your life before it's absolutely necessary! ...."

And then, when she realized suddenly how near she had been to actually uttering those words, panic seized her, and she wrenched her glance away, and looked round wildly as if seeking for something to distract her.

Dr. Fernandez dropped his own glance to the carpet, and staring at it he said quietly:

"Then that is settled. You will remain with Gia? You will accept it that I am quite satisfied with you?"

"Y-yes — if you really are satisfied."

"There are no 'ifs' about it."

"Thank you," she murmured, barely audibly, and he reached for a cigarette-box and selected and lighted a cigarette.

"You may find it a little dull here with only Señora Cortina and her husband, but at least your time will be your own." He looked up at her quickly, as much as to say: "And I suppose you'll spend it with Peter Hamilton-Tracey!"

She said quickly, remembering Peter's aunt's invitation:

"I wouldn't find it at all dull here, but, as it happens, I have received an invitation to Madrid also. Miss Tracey has a flat in Madrid, and she wondered whether perhaps I could get a few days off and stay with her."

Once again he frowned.

"Were you going to ask for those few days?"

"I wouldn't have done so, but now that my services are not going to be required for a week at least it does seem an opportunity. ...."

Her voice faded away, and he asked in rather an odd voice — certainly rather a cold voice:

"To see Madrid, or to accompany Miss Tracey and her nephew on sight-seeing expeditions?"

"I am not at all sure that Peter will be there."

"Really?" rather dryly. "But as he appears to be a free agent I feel quite certain he will be there!"

'You have no objections to my staying with Miss Tracey?"

He shrugged his elegant shoulders slightly.

"On the contrary, I suppose I should be grateful that she will prevent your being dull. And, as a matter of fact, although I don't know Miss Tracey personally, I do know of her. She has established quite a reputation as an artist, I believe, and is a welcome visitor in the homes of many of my friends. It is high time I myself got to know her, and I will ask her to dinner before we leave. Where is she staying in San Cecilio?"

Lisa told him, "The Carabela."

Once again their eyes met for rather longer than an instant, and a queer little smile slid into his.

"Do you remember when you stayed there?" he asked her.

"I remember perfectly."

"And the night when your shoe caught in the cobbles of the jetty!" He looked away deliberately, as if forcing himself to do so. "It will be nice for you to stay with Miss Tracey," he said, "and we must certainly have her to dinner. From what I know of her she is an ideal person to show you Madrid."

But Lisa thought sadly, did it really matter who showed her Madrid, when he would not be the one? If *he* showed her Madrid! . . .

Then her breath caught, and once again she had the terrifying conviction that she was near to betraying herself to him, and she determined from that moment to be extra specially careful.

She was glad when he suddenly nodded and said:

122

"Very well, Miss Waring, you may go!"

And although she knew herself dismissed, she went gladly because it was a relief to escape.

CHAPTER ELEVEN

GIA wasn't at all pleased when she learned that she was to spend a week, possibly a fortnight, as the guest of Doña Beatriz in Madrid, without either Lisa or her father to give her some support.

To Lisa it was disturbing that the doctor's small daughter had such a firmly rooted dislike of Doña Beatriz. That part of her training devoted to the psychology of the child mind had prepared her for the unreasonable attitudes sometimes taken up by the young towards people they encountered, or sets of circumstances; but it hadn't been a lengthy enough training to give her any real idea how to cope with such unreasonable attitudes when they occurred within her own experience. And most people would have said that Gia's attitude to Doña Beatriz was unreasonable, for the latter went out of her way to be as nice as she knew how to her, and part of her policy to win her esteem in the past had been to load her with presents.

The box of expensive chocolates on their arrival at the villa, followed by many other things, was evidence of this policy. The many attempts to woo Gia away from her English governess and take her for walks, and talks; the constant supervision of her wardrobe, and the ever-open eye to things relating to her physical well-being, were other pieces of evidence. That Gia persisted in disliking her, that she shrank from being alone with her, and that — as Lisa knew — she mistrusted her, were sufficient proofs that her policy was failing, and that it looked like being a complete waste of effort.

Which alarmed Lisa when she thought of the child's future, and wondered how she would get through life with a stepmother for whom she had so little time, even if her father, apparently, had a great deal. At the moment Doña Beatriz could not do much in the way of displaying that she was hurt, and perhaps puzzled, by the plain little girl's dislike. But later on, when she was Dr. Feranandez' second wife, and secure in her position as mistress of his home and his household, then the situation would be different. Then it might be *very different*!

It was the thought of how soon things might change, and get out of hand for Gia, that frightened Lisa, and she wondered whether it should be part of her policy to re-orientate the child's mind where her future stepmother was concerned. But, even if it was, she wouldn't know how to go about it, not being a strictly impartial governess. And she was confirmed in her own secret unhappiness because Gia herself was so certain that Doña Beatriz would one day become her stepmother.

"Everybody says so," she said more than once to Lisa, and the English girl wondered how many servants had been talking in the child's hearing, or whether being Spanish she was precocious where such matters were concerned. Or whether it was purely instinct.

Another reason why Gia viewed the prospect of returning to Madrid with Doña Beatriz with something like dismay was because she didn't want to leave the coast. Madrid, as she was probably aware, would be sizzling with heat at that season of the year, and Lisa was surprised that her father should consent to her leaving behind her the more bracing airs of the Costa Brava for a reason that seemed inadequate, particularly in view of the fact that she had so recently been seriously ill. A dental appointment was no doubt important, but if it was only a check-up it might surely have been postponed for a while longer, when Gia would have benefited still more from her sojourn on the coast. And the fact that it was not being postponed was a very clear indication of the hold Doña Beatriz had managed to secure over the doctor's domestic affairs, and possibly over his own more reasonable instincts.

"You will be here when I come back, won't you?" Gia said anxiously, while Lisa packed for her. "Promise me you'll be here when I come back?" reaching out and grasping at Lisa as if she was suddenly afraid.

Lisa folded a little silk suit, and smiled at her.

"I'll be here," she promised. "At least, I'll be here when you come back."

"You're not going to stay here?"

"I might see something of you in Madrid," Lisa half promised, perhaps unwisely. "Your father has given me permission to spend a few days with a friend, and as she also lives in Madrid we might possibly meet."

But Gia looked at her with uncannily shrewd eyes for a child.

"I don't think Doña Beatriz would like that," she said.

Lisa glanced at her quickly, and then away.

"You don't think Doña Beatriz approves of our association?"

"I think she will be happy when — when I go away to school, and you go away too!"

Lisa made certain that the locks of the suitcase were secure, and then she rose from her knees and went and sat beside Gia in the window-seat. It was a wide window-seat, padded, and made comfortable with cushions, and Gia often curled up there. Today Lisa thought she looked almost painfully thin and undersized for her years, and in spite of the light coating of tan she had acquired in recent weeks her naturally sallow complexion showed up, and it made her one beautiful feature, her heavily-lashed eyes, look large and shadow-haunted.

"How do you feel about going away to school?" Lisa asked, certain in her own mind that the child was too young, and too badly prepared, for a boarding-school, especially in a country, where she would feel utterly strange.

Gia clutched at her again, and this time Lisa drew her close to her, and the dark head dropped upon her shoulder.

"I don't want to go away to school," was the whispered confession. "At least——"

"Yes?"

'It wouldn't be so bad in England if you were there! Will you be there?' '

Lisa stroked the ragged elf-locks mechanically.

"I don't really know. That is, I'm not quite sure what my future plans will be."

"But if you're there will you come and see me?"

"Of course! Oh, of course!"

For several seconds they sat silent, and Lisa knew an acutely despairing sensation, because Gia's future was no affair of hers.

"Do you know what I wish?" Gia asked, in a dreamy voice, at last, as she stared out through the window at the blue of the sea.

"No. Tell me," Lisa requested.

Gia put back her head and looked up at her.

"I wish that my papa would marry you! I wish that you would stay with us — that you would go back with us to Madrid — and that Doña Beatriz would go away somewhere where we need never see her again!"

Before Lisa could make any sort of reply to this — and the childish confession robbed her, temporarily, of the power to assemble words—the door behind them opened, and Dr. Fernandez quietly entered the room. He looked at them both for a long moment in silence, the expression in his eyes neither enigmatic nor surprised, but still unreadable, and Lisa had no idea at all whether he had overheard his daughter's words. But the thoughts that he could have overheard them all but petrified her.

"I saw your friend, Miss Tracey, at the Carabela this morning," he said, advancing into the room. "Although it's rather short notice, she has consented to dine with us tonight — she and, of course, her nephew."

"Oh, yes," Lisa heard herself saying, her color coming and going so rapidly that he looked at her keenly.

"It will be a change for you to have your English friends share a meal with us."

"Yes," she agreed.

Gia had made no move towards him, and he carelessly flicked her cheek.

"You look rather sad," he said. "In fact, you both look rather sad! Is it because of the imminence of this parting between you?"

Gia answered in a small, hollow voice:

"I wish that Lisa was coming with me to Madrid!"

"Lisa will be waiting for you here when you return — and by rights you should call her Miss Waring."

"She prefers that I call her Lisa. Isn't that so?" once more putting back her head and appealing to her governess for confirmation.

"That is so." And Lisa suddenly ignored his presence and hugged Gia to her again.

"In that case, there is no real reason why I should not say Lisa, also!" He sat down on the window-seat not far away from them, and looked at them both quizzically. "It would seem that you are a very devoted pair, and you look a little hopeless in this evening light — and young!" His eyes brooded on them rather strangely. "Very young!"

"Lisa is twenty-four," Gia told him, although he already knew as much, "and Señora Cortina says that twenty-four is too old for a woman still unmarried. I heard her tell Señor Cortina so."

"Really?" The quizzical look returned. "For a little pitcher you certainly have very long ears, and they should never incline in the direction of backstairs gossip. Hasn't Lisa told you that?"

"I——" Lisa began, but his smile at her was suddenly impish.

"How do you feel about this problem of being still unmarried, Miss Waring? Although I suppose in England twenty-four is hardly an age when you begin to look forward to spinsterhood? There are still several years for enjoyment, before domestic problems need claim you!"

"Are domestic problems an inevitable part of marriage?" Lisa asked quietly.

"They seem invariably to arise — even in Spain!" he admitted.

"And enjoyment flies out of the window when those problems do arise? — as love does, according to a saying we have at home, when poverty enters the door!"

"It is hardly the same sort of enjoyment as unfettered youth approves of."

"But the opinion of unfettered youth is hardly a yardstick for the rest of one's adult life!" She looked down at the fingers of one of her hands, entwined in Gia's small fingers. "And problems, when shared, should become less. If properly shared, I have been given to understand, they disappear altogether."

"Sometimes," he agreed, "that is so, but it is by no means always so," and his voice was suddenly harsh.

She looked up at him, as if his change of tone intrigued her.

"And when it is not so," she insisted, "disillusionment is the result?"

It could not have been so in his own case, she felt certain. But it could have been so in his experience of other people's lives — as a medical man.

"Disillusionment is a very unpleasant and ugly word," he said, and he stood up and walked away from the brightness of the window, and Gia's voice followed him.

"I don't want Lisa to go away, Papa! I don't want her *ever* to go away!"

Lisa felt her face flame, and she gave Gia's fingers a tight, warning squeeze to prevent her saying anything further.

But Gia was determined to continue with her appeal.

"Please, Papa! . . ."

He turned and came back to them, and his dark, handsome face was set in lines of unusual gravity. In his lustrous eyes was a kind of deep and spreading sombreness as he ruffled his daughter's elf-locks.

"Who is talking of Lisa going away? It is you who are going back to Madrid for a few days, and as a matter of fact Lisa will be there, too, and perhaps——"

"Yes Papa?" eagerly.

"Oh, nothing. . . . Nothing that we can plan. We will see." He actually smiled into the small girl's eyes, and his hand on her head was very gentle. "Miss Waring — and you must not get me into the habit of making use of her Christian name, because she might not approve! — will probably have plans of her own, and there is no reason why they should include a child like you!"

Lisa was about to protest almost as eagerly as her charge that any plans she made in Madrid could certainly be elastic enough to include Gia, but a sudden look of cold formality overspread his face, and she realized that the brief period of intimacy that had linked the three of them was over. Over and would probably never occur again! All in a moment he was very much her employer.

"Miss Waring, you mustn't let my daughter make unreasonable demands upon you," he said, "and while you are in Madrid I hope you will do better things than arrange meetings with a small girl. You are young, and Madrid can be quite gay, even in a temperature that will probably defeat you a little, at any rate at first. And it is absurd for the pair of you to behave as if you are parting for ever! You will meet again in a very short while. But it will be as well if you bear it in mind that the final parting will have to come!"

Once more he ruffled his daughter's hair.

"You will have to get used to that idea, *chiquita*! Do you understand?"

"Yes, Papa!" she barely whispered.

He didn't look at Lisa again before he walked out, and she felt quite certain as the door closed upon him that he had overheard his daughter's impulsively expressed wish when he entered the room. And that was his way of letting them both know that the notion was not one that appealed even to his sense of humor.

"It will be as well if you bear it in mind that the final parting will have to come! . . ."

That night Miss Tracey and her nephew dined at the villa, and it was a matter of surprise to Lisa that Miss Tracey got on extremely well with her host, and that they seemed to have quite a lot in common, and a number of things they found interesting to discuss.

While Doña Beatriz engaged Peter in spritely conversation, Dr. Fernandez and Aunt Grizel ranged over such varied subjects as art and world politics, travel and the value of universal language for drawing people together; and after dinner they continued the conversation in the glassed-in verandah, while the stars shone almost frostily in the night sky outside, and the sea murmured at the foot of the garden.

Aunt Grizel wore a dress of black lace which made her look unexpectedly distinguished, and as her jewellery was good it was a distinction that was backed up by a suggestion of considerable affluence. She seemed to know so many of the right people — the people Dr. Fernandez knew — and her knowledge of Spain and Spanish ways was inexhaustible. Her enthusiasm for Spain was apparently unquenchable.

"I am looking forward to having Miss Waring stay with me," she said. "I shall show her such a lot!"

"And your nephew will help you to show her all that we feel she ought to see?" Doña Beatriz interposed, with a charming smile.

"Peter?" Miss Tracey looked a little surprised. "As to that, I can't say. . . . Peter may follow us to Madrid." She looked more quizzically at her nephew, and then at Lisa. "Yes; I think it very likely he will follow us!" she admitted.

Dr. Fernandez bent towards her with his cigarette-case, containing the long thin cigarettes she so enjoyed.

"I think it is almost certain Miss Waring will have someone to escort her in Madrid," he said, with a suavity in his voice that caused her to look at him for the first time in surprise; and then she looked quickly at Doña Beatriz, who was presiding gracefully behind the tray of coffee-cups, and once more at her nephew, who was frowning ever so slightly.

"Yes," she said emphatically, as if she had all at once quite made up her mind. "I think you are right, Doctor. I shall insist on Peter coming with us to Madrid, and he shall escort us both — myself as well as Lisa. We will combine to give Lisa a really good time — to make her feel young and carefree for the first time in her life!" Her eyes dwelt thoughtfully on the slender, silent figure of the girl. "And you know, my dear," she added, "I don't think you've ever been really young and carefree before, although you look so very young. Peter says it has been other people's children for a year or so now, and that is a year or so too early when you've hardly lived yourself. You want a little interlude of freedom!"

She shifted her glance to her host.

"Don't you agree with me, Doctor, that *that* is what Lisa really wants?"

CHAPTER TWELVE

BUT BEFORE they went to Madrid they spent a couple of days in a small fishing village farther along the coast, where Miss Tracey did some painting. She told Lisa that the village had impressed her the first time she saw it, and that she had always wanted to capture on canvas the simple charm of the fishing-boats drawn up on the beach, and the way the coast curved into an inlet at that point.

Once Gia had departed in her father's car, with Doña Beatriz wearing the serene air of one in charge of an expedition, Lisa had felt almost painfully eager to get away from the villa, and although the fishing village was no real change of scenery, Miss Tracey was a welcome change of companionship, for she, too, was serene, in a much pleasanter way than Doña Beatriz, and there was something about her that filled Lisa with confidence.

She didn't feel any longer like the paid governess. She felt as if her presence was wanted by someone who was taking an interest in her for a reason that was highly flattering, because it could mean that she enjoyed her society. For if she didn't she certainly wouldn't have put herself out to give her this little holiday when, but for her offer to do so, Lisa would have been left alone at the villa with only Señora Cortina and her husband — and the puppy she had rescued! — for company.

Not that she wouldn't have been able to bear that; but without Gia *and* her father . . .!

Miss Tracey gave her rather a careful scrutiny when she came down to dinner that first evening in the small hotel where they had booked for a couple of nights; and then she remarked:

"That's a very pretty frock you're wearing, my dear." Actually it was the plain ivory taffeta with the poppies surrounding the skirt that Lisa had worn on what she thought was her last night in San Cecilio. "But you should have pretty things at your age. There are some wonderful shops in Madrid, and we'll have a real shopping burst when we get there, shall we?"

But Lisa looked dubious.

"I haven't a great deal of money . . ." she was beginning, when Aunt Grizel interrupted her, reaching across the table and laying a hand on hers.

"Of course you haven't! Not when all you receive is a governess's salary! And even if it's a generous salary, it won't go far in Madrid. But I'll tell you something, shall I?"

Lisa looked at her expectantly.

"I'm a vulgarly wealthy woman — and I really mean vulgarly! One day it will all go to Peter (and I think that's one reason why, knowing that his future is taken care of, he puts off looking for serious employment!) But that's no reason why we shouldn't spend some of it between us, you and I. I never married, so of course I never had a daughter, or knew any of the delights of dressing her up for a party. But if you'd only let me have the happiness I *could* dress you up!"

Lisa gaped at her.

"But—but what for?" she stammered.

Grizelda Tracey smiled.

"For all the fun and jollification that lies ahead! My dear, I'm going to warn you — Madrid will cook you at this season of the year, but the nights are wonderful! If you've never seen Spanish stars over Madrid, then you've something to wait for."

"I've seen them over San Cecilio," Lisa got in, a little breathlessly.

"Yes, my dear, you've seen them over San Cecilio — and San Cecilio is highly romantic, and the stars make you dream dreams. But in Madrid the dreams come true! Or it is possible for them to come true! Therefore the stars are that much brighter. Wait until you see them!"

Once again she lightly touched the girl's hand.

"I know a lot of people in Madrid. It is not like Paris, but the shop-window displays will make you think of Paris, and the women are smart. Madrileñas are *all* smart! There are enough beauty parlors to ensure that no one looks really plain, and you and I will visit one of them! I'm not suggesting that you need a visit to a beauty parlor, but I do — it's something I've secretly wanted to do all my life, but never had the courage! And with you I think I'll find the courage. And then we'll do that shopping, and then I'll get in touch with my friends. A good many of them will be away just now, of course, but enough will remain. . . . And Peter shall take us to shows, and night-clubs — yes; we'll visit a night-club! You must see *flamenco*! My dear, even an old woman like me gets excited at the sight of *flamenco*, and as soon as I hear castanets I feel the most extraordinary sensation creeping over me!"

She went on talking this way, and Lisa listened until she felt bemused. But although the programme sounded almost too much for one whose life had flowed in such a narrow channel from the moment she was born, she wouldn't have been twenty-four if it hadn't quickened her blood just to listen to Miss Tracey talking, and the only thing she insisted on when she got an opportunity to speak was that she should pay for any purchases she made.

To which Miss Tracey replied:

"You can pay for the odds and ends — *I'll* supply the essentials. Not only for you, but for

136

me as well. These old tweeds," looking down at them, "make me feel like a grandmother!" And then she chuckled. "Which I shall never be!"

Peter arrived in Madrid ahead of them, and although his aunt had given him permission to install himself in a modest hotel, when he met them off the train he explained, with a twinkle in his very blue eyes, that all the modest hotels had been full, and he had had to put up at one of Madrid's leading, and distinctly palatial, edifices.

Aunt Grizel shook her head at him.

"Do you think I'm a millionairess?" she demanded. "And do you think I'm easily deceived? You took a taxi straight to the Bahia Palace, and there you intend to remain so long as Lisa remains in Madrid! Well, well . . . I suppose it won't altogether ruin me!"

"As a matter of fact," Peter said, the audacious twinkle remaining in his eyes as he took both their arms and led them straight to a taxi. "I can't think why the two of you don't join me at the Bahia Palace. That flat of yours is a bit cramped, Aunt Grizel!——

"Cramped or not," she returned, "it will do for us!" Then she looked up at him approvingly. "However, you look very nice" — and he did look almost elegant in his well-pressed lounge-suit, and flowing Eton tie — "and I've no doubt I shall receive quite a number of bills as a result of your visit to Madrid. But as I want you to look nice to escort us around I won't be really cross with you."

"Thanks." He squeezed her arm, apparently having no conscience at all about using her credit, and then almost tenderly assisted Lisa into the taxi.

Once arrived at the flat, which was at the top of a tall modern block, further evidence of his extravagance awaited them. The flat was full of flowers, spicy carnations and dark red and yellow roses. The yellow roses were in the room he had assumed Lisa would occupy. The red roses were in the lounge.

Aunt Grizel touched them with a faint look of amusement on her face once she got over the surprise of being greeted by these floral offerings — to be paid for, no doubt, by herself!

"Why didn't you put the red roses in Lisa's room?" she asked. "The yellow ones would have done for the lounge."

Her quizzical look made him grin, and Lisa flushed delicately.

"I didn't want to appear to be rushing things!" Peter explained, and the way he looked at Lisa made her flush still more.

"This afternoon I have plans," he said. "Lisa is coming out to tea with me first of all——"

"Nothing of the sort!" his aunt told him. "I, too, have plans, and the first part of them involves getting on to the telephone and making some apointments. And after that we have shopping to do."

"No one shops in the Spanish capital in the afternoon, as you very well know," Peter replied imperturbably. "It is the time for *siesta*."

"It will come awake when we want it to do so," Miss Tracey assured him. "And we haven't had our lunch yet. I suppose you'll stay to lunch! Or does the Bahia Palace cater for your tastes better than my Juanita is likely to do?"

Peter stayed to lunch.

"My Juanita" was one of the reasons why Lisa's visit to Madrid was such a success from the first. Juanita was the ideal cook-housekeeper, and she had been with Miss Tracey for several years. She was plump and good-looking in a typically Spanish way, a wonderful cook, even-tempered, methodical and punctual — which was not typically Spanish — and she adored Miss Tracey. It was she who had arranged the flowers, and she had thought the yellow roses very suitable for the young *señorita* who, being English, probably had hair to match them. And she was not disappointed.

That night, when she brushed it out — a task she insisted on — she exclaimed in delight at the fineness of its texture, and the silken softness of it.

"Like moonlight!" she said, and watched it ripple about Lisa's shoulders with charmed eyes. And when her employer mentioned the beauty parlor she snorted. "For you, perhaps, señorita — at your age it is good not to neglect the looks! — but for the Señorita Waring, no! She has no need of beauty parlors!"

Nevertheless, since Miss Tracey had made the appointment, Lisa found herself accompanying her next day to an up-to-the-minute salon where a few recognizable improvements were made to the manner in which she wore her hair, and as a result of skilled attention it discovered an extra sheen which even Juanita had to admit had not been there before. And her nails were attended to, and she came away with a whole series of new cosmetics that had been selected to blend with her skin. As for Miss Tracey, she came away with the lavender-blue hair-rinse that she had always secretly wished to see transfiguring her snowy locks, and the first lipstick she had ever possessed in her life.

"I probably shan't use it," she said; "but it will give me confidence just to know it's there in my handbag, and that I can produce it in a sophisticated way if I feel like it."

After that they went shopping, and that night Peter took them both out to dinner wearing entirely new additions to their wardrobes. In Lisa's case it was oyster-pink net with a series of underskirts that rustled when she moved, and a tiny bodice that made the most of her absurdly slender proportions, and in Miss Tracey's pearl-grey satin. She had never worn satin in her life before, considering it too opulent for her proportions, which were decidedly stocky; and when Lisa persuaded her to drape a rich petunia stole about her shoulders she wondered whether she was permitting her emancipation to be too sudden.

A more gradual attempt to acquire something in the nature of elderly glamor might have suited her better, she thought; Lisa was enthusiastic about the results.

"It's quite a transformation!" she declared. And then, afraid that she sounded rude, she added: "You could have done this years ago, but you never bothered. You stuck to your tweeds, and you're not really the type for tweeds. You can be really elegant, dressed to suit your type!"

Aunt Grizel laughed, as if genuinely amused, and then pinched the cheek of the girl affectionately.

"Well, we're in this together, my dear. And you look like the fairy on the Christmas tree in that gauzy thing! I'd never describe you as elegant, but I do think you're quite enchanting! Wait until the dark Spanish heads start turning round rapidly when you make your appearance — masculine heads, of course, I mean!" She went to her dressing-table and lifted the stopper from a flagon of expensive perfume. "You must have a dab of this behind your ears, and in the appropriate places. Maybe it's a bit heavy, but Madrileñas love heavy perfume, and the girl in that beauty parlor place assured me it was madly provocative — *apasionado* perfume she called it!"

But Lisa declined it, thinking she was hardly the type to carry off *apasionado* perfumes, and Aunt Grizel, replacing the stopper reluctantly, nevertheless agreed with her.

"Well, perhaps you're right, We'll have to get you something a trifle more redolent of violets, or an English rose-garden." She did not notice how Lisa stiffened slightly at the mention of rose-gardens, and then looked unconsciously wistful. "But don't forget to wear this," picking up a stole of fine black lace, that was the perfect complement to the pink net dress, and draping it about Lisa's shoulders.

And as they went out together she thought:

"The girl isn't merely lovely — she's like a Dresden-china rose!"

The evening passed off in an unreal and slightly light-headed fashion for Lisa. Peter quite obviously shared his aunt's opinion of their young fellow-countrywoman once he had an opportunity to examine her in the lights of the exclusive restaurant to which he took them, and because it was such an exclusive restaurant, without any guitar-playing or clicking of castanets between the courses, Lisa was a little misled about Madrid on that first evening that she dined out in it.

The champagne they consumed — which Peter insisted upon — was of the very highest quality; the food was delicious, and wonderfully served; the rest of the diners looked as elegant as Miss Tracey's grey satin dress, and the atmosphere was as quiet and orderly as a pool. But it was not the Madrid of the throbbing interludes, the *"apasionado"* perfumes, the clashing tambourines. There were no whirling skirts, or roses caught up in mantillas, or dark eyes peering seductively over the tops of fans.

"Another night," Peter said, when she mentioned her surprise at finding so much restraint. "This is Madrid *par excellence*! I thought it better to introduce you gradually. Begin at the top, and work downwards!" He grinned at her.

She thought, Madrid *par excellence* — the sort of background against which Gia's father, and

Doña Beatriz, probably moved, when they were in their home city. And suddenly she thought: "Supposing they walked in now!"

But they didn't walk in, and the dinner pursued its leisurely course. When it was over, and the final liqueur and coffee had been consumed and appreciated, and it seemed very late, they walked part of the way back to Aunt Grizel's flat because it was such a breathlessly hot and perfect night, and it seemed a sin to take a taxi.

Aunt Grizel drew Lisa's attention to the stars that seemed to be blazing fitfully down on them through the sensuously warm atmosphere, and she said:

"There they are! Stars over Madrid! . . . Aren't they huge?"

Lisa looked up at them. They were wondrous stars, but they were not the stars that peered at their reflections in the indigo waste of waters that washed upon the shores of her beloved San Cecilio— San Cecilio, where she had sat in a little café on the waterfront one night, and drunk wine with her present employer. Wine the color of ripe apricots, and as clear as glass. . . . .

It had gone to her head a little that night, that apricot-colored wine. . . . Or else the offer of a position she had never expected had gone to her head! And she had been very unwise to accept. She should have gone home the following day, and in that way she would have avoided heartache in the future — for the whole of her future!

And even now, after such a pleasant evening, she felt the coldness settling round her heart, the loneliness because here in this impressive capital city of Spain was one man who could easily get on without her for the rest of his life, and very shortly now would pay her a final month's salary — with perhaps a little over as a kind of bonus — and tell her her services were no longer required.

She stumbled, and Peter caught hold of her slim, bare elbow, and gripped it rather tightly.

"Tomorrow," he said, in a warm, intimate tone, "I'll have lots more to show you, Lisa. It's going to be a wonderful week or fortnight! And I think we ought to make it a fortnight! Fernandez and that odd infant of his can do without you for that length of time!"

Which was another reason why she suddenly felt as if a knife turned in her heart.

143

CHAPTER THIRTEEN

BUT THE TEN days that passed with the rapidity
of lightning were undeniabably enjoyable days for
Lisa.

They began in the same manner each morning,
with Juanita bringing her early tea — Miss
Tracey was not one of those people who lived
abroad and forewent any of the privileges of being
a British citizen, and tea-drinking was an in-
grained habit with her — and then following
it up with a breakfast tray containing orange
juice and curls of crisp bacon and toast. After
that Miss Tracey made her appearance in a bathrobe, and they talked about all sorts of things,
including the plans for that day, and what Peter
had decided upon, and what he had decided could
be postponed for yet another day.

So far he had taken her on a whirlwind sight-
seeing tour of Madrid. She had seen the Escorial
Palace, and the Royal Palace — El Pardo, a
delightful residence enhanced by magnificent
woods, which Velasquez used as a background
to his portraits. She had seen the Prado Museum
and other museums, churches, fashionable
thoroughfares, fountain-decorated avenues. She
had sipped iced drinks in gay open-air cafés, and
lunched in impressive restaurants; and at cocktail
time, or "Vermouth time", an hour when most
other capitals were sitting down to dinner, she
and Miss Tracey had been introduced to one or
two discreet little bars, where the atmosphere was
very fashionable, and very respectable, and they,
too, had become part of the background, and it
had seemed that such a thing as a dinner hour
would never be arrived at.

For dinner was always late in Spain, and time
seemed to have no importance whatever. It just

drifted by. And after dinner there were the fashionable cabarets; in particular one, where the décor was positively sumptuous, where the famous *flamenco* songs were sung, and Lisa had her first taste of the sort of thing that charms the tourists, and puts money into the pockets of Madrileño night-club proprietors.

Lisa, like Miss Tracey, felt something like excitement creep over her when she heard the clicking castanets, and saw the billowing dresses and the wildly voluptuous movements of the Andalusian entertainers for the first time. The second time it still thrilled, but not quite so wildly. She much preferred lingering in the fragrant avenues afterwards, on the way home, breathing the first breath of coolness since morning dawned, seeing the yellow glow of a lantern in a silent, dignified courtyard, and hearing the whisper of the plane trees that flanked the just as silent squares.

Then there were still shopping expeditions, and it was a little disturbing how much money she spent, because she declined to allow her very generous hostess to do more than make her a few very generous presents. And that seemed to put her hopelessly in the debt of Miss Tracey, whom she grew to like very much indeed.

Peter she had always liked, and he improved on continuous acquaintance. A year before, when she had met him for the first time in the Hamilton-Tracey house, she would never have believed that one day he would behave towards her as if she had an irresistible attraction for him — and that was another thing that bothered her, because he would never have an irresistible attraction for her.

Only one man would ever have that!

Miss Tracey certainly seemed to have quite a few friends who remained in Madrid. Several of them came to tea, and one particularly charming family with a handsome young son named Ricardo gave a party to celebrate some member of the family's birthday, and Aunt Grizel and her English guest and her nephew were all three invited.

Aunt Grizel had been right in one of her predictions. Dark, masculine heads did swing round abruptly when Lisa became part of a mixed gathering, and her striking fairness seemed to arouse admiration almost immediately. Ricardo Espinhaco took one look at her and capitulated at once, and throughout the whole of the evening, while the celebrations for the birthday went on, he remained at her side, and even Peter found it well-nigh impossible to dislodge him.

The party was held at one of Madrid's gayer, but still highly reputable restaurants, and it was a very lavish party, with toasts drunk in champagne, as well as champagne cocktails to get everyone into the right frame of mind. There seemed to be endless uncles and aunts and cousins, as well as guests, and Lisa estimated that the party would cost Papa Espinhaco quite a large sum of money. But money was plainly one thing that didn't trouble that particular family. The women's dresses were nothing short of superb, while their dazzling displays of jewellery took her breath away when she first saw them. Even the younger girls sparkled like a display window of a fabulous jeweller's shop; but they were extremely nice young girls — in fact, the whole family was nice — and Lisa was greatly attracted to them.

It was Ricardo who became a bit of an embarrassment, for his admiration was so unconcealed, and he used every sort of persuasive argument to remain near her throughout the evening.

"I have not known many English girls, and not one who looked quite like you," he told her, his black eyes resting almost caressingly on her fairness. "You are like a combination of moonlight and an English spring. . . . I have been once to England in the springtime, and I know that it is a little like you!" He touched her pink net dress, which she was wearing for the occasion. "This makes you look like a flower, *señorita!*" he told her.

Lisa looked faintly amused, although not being accustomed to these fulsome flatteries she was also a little embarrassed.

"Moonlight, and an English spring, and a flower at the same time!" she murmured. "I must be quite a combination!"

"You are indeed,'" he assured her, seeking to touch her hand as they sat side by side at the large flower-decked table given over to the party. "You are all things that I have sometimes dreamed about! . . . I must see you, *señorita* — more of you, I mean! — while you remain in Madrid. You must permit me to escort you sometimes! You will, won't you?" he pleaded, his shapely olive fingers reaching more determinedly for her hand, which, however, she snatched away. "Please, *señorita!*" he begged.

The lights had just gone up again after a floor show, and some of the enthusiastic younger ones had started to dance on the glistening ballroom floor. It was Peter who came to Lisa's rescue, leaping quickly to his feet and all but snatching her off her chair and saying briskly:

"Come on, Lisa, let's dance!"

As they circled the floor he remarked on an obvious note of displeasure:

"These Spaniards don't lose any time, do they? But that young man Ricardo is a fast worker even for a Spaniard! Has he been successful in dating you up yet? I noticed his mama was looking anxious when she was watching the two of you a short while ago! Most of these young men have their futures already planned for them, you know, and no doubt she was sensing difficulty later on — when the time draws near for Ricardo to settle down! — if he got involved with anyone like you! Not part of the pre-arranged plan, if you know what I mean."

Lisa answered coolly.

"Señora Espinhaco need have no fears. Her son is perfectly safe where I am concerned."

Peter grinned down at her with something sceptical about the grin, nevertheless.

"You could be swept off your feet! These Latin types are rather like inflammable matches — the non-safety type. They ignite suddenly, and the rest of the box goes, too!"

"I am not in the least likely to go too," Lisa said, frowning at the top of his shoulder because the subject of arranged Spanish marriages was not one she found at all palatable just then. She didn't want to think of Spanish marriages at all — certainly not arranged ones! — and the cold-blooded manner in which the partners set about things (or permitted their relatives to set about them) made her feel almost angry. She was certain that it would be a marriage of expediency if Dr. Fernandez married Doña Beatriz, and not because he was in love with her, attractive woman though she was.

Why she was so certain of this she couldn't be sure, but she was sure of it.

When she first caught sight of him and Doña Beatriz, standing between Señor and Señora Espinhaco, within a few feet of their table, she could hardly believe her eyes. The evening had spent itself, and sambas and tangos had followed sambas and tangos, as well as more intricate Cuban dances, and Lisa was feeling a little exhausted, because she had never once been without a partner. She wondered whether exhaustion was causing her to see things that were not actually there when she caught her first glimpse of the doctor. She had seen him several times now in white tie and tails, and she might easily have conjured him up out of sheer concentrated dwelling upon him even when she was with other people, and she hadn't heard a word of him for days.

For there had been no messages for her, no inquiries, no information as to what was happening to Gia, or when they were to return to the coast. She had written to Gia twice — little, affectionate notes, which had not actually called for any answer — and she had sent her a small present in the shape of a novelty for her dressing-table, but none of these had been acknowledged, and she had been feeling concern because of the persistent silence.

But now— and without any doubt he was there in the flesh, and not just a figment of her imagination — her employer, as well as the woman who proposed to marry him, were standing between her own host and hostess, being plainly welcomed by them, although such late additions to the party, and Miss Tracey was in the group, too, looking complacent in her pearl-grey satin, and as her partner led her up to the group Lisa could hear her say:

"Oh, yes, Lisa is thoroughly enjoying Madrid. Aren't you, my dear?" stretching forth a hand to her, as Lisa reached her side. "So thoroughly that I don't believe she's had a moment to herself the whole of the evening!"

Her eyes beamed at Lisa with so much satisfaction that Lisa felt it was almost unnatural, but Dr. Fernandez was surveying her without any expression at all on his face. His eyes were slightly narrowed, his mouth and chin rather sternly and ascetically set, in spite of the fact that his hostess had just been gushing all over him, and assuring him that she perfectly understood the reason why he was late. The important thing was that he had managed to find some time to devote to them — he and Doña Beatriz, and she beamed round on the lovely redhead as if it was very well understood that she had to be included in any transports that were poured out over Dr. Fernandez.

But Doña Beatriz's eyes were at that moment for Lisa, and Lisa alone — unless it was the oyster-pink net that was billowing round her. Lisa's slim and creamy neck was encircled by a row of finely graded pearls that belonged to Miss Tracey, and which the latter had insisted on her wearing for the occasion — "They're insured, my dear, so don't worry too much if disaster overtakes you and you lose them!" she had declared —and her hair had been cut rather short, and framed her face in a soft aureole of gold. She looked young and rather touchingly lovely, but poised and in complete command of herself at the same time, and the look she directed at Doña Beatriz was neither subservient nor surprised. In fact, it was for the first time cool and withdrawn.

"You *look* as if you're enjoying yourself, Miss Waring," Doña Beatriz remarked, with condescension in her tone. "In fact, you look as if you haven't wasted a moment of your time in Madrid, and used up quite a bit of your salary!

Lisa made no reply to this, but turned to the doctor.

"How is Gia?" she asked.

He returned her level look with a distant one of his own.

"Gia is quite well."

"I wondered how she was getting on. I was a little anxious about her."

"If you were anxious you could have satisfied your anxiety with a simple inquiry."

"I have written twice and received no reply to either of my letters, and I also sent her a present which it was not necessary to acknowledge," she told him with a slight stiffening of her slender figure. ,

At that his eyebrows ascended in the way she knew so well, and Doña Beatriz interposed somewhat hurriedly:

"Yes; that is quite right, Julio, but I'm afraid Gia has been so caught up in a whirl of unusual excitements that she hasn't had either the time or inclination to bother about answering anyone's letters. But it was naughty of her not to acknowledge Miss Waring's present, and I'll mention it to her."

"Don't bother," Lisa said, the stiffness in her voice this time. "It was only a very trifling present, and one doesn't expect a child of that age to bother about writing formal letters of thanks. But I thought I might have had some sort of message to indicate that she was well, or even that she was looking forward to returning to the coast."

"You don't think that she might so much enjoy her stay with me that she wouldn't even think about returning to the coast?" Doña Beatriz inquired, a trifle icily.

Lisa looked at her coolly.

"The coast is a child's natural playground at this time of the year, and Gia is a very normal child. And Madrid is hardly a change for her. But so long as she is happy that is all I care about."

"An admirable sentiment on the part of a governess, I'm sure," Doña Beatriz remarked, and people standing round looked at Lisa in faint surprise, as if for the first time they were seeing her in the role of a governess — or that was the impression she received.

Peter, who was at her elbow, suddenly touched her on the arm and smiled at her.

"They're playing a waltz," he said, "the first of the evening. So come along and remember that you're *not* a governess at the moment."

"Dear Peter!" she thought, as she slipped easily into his arms, and their steps matched perfectly. "I don't believe he likes Doña Beatriz any more than I do! . . . But not for the same reason that I feel I could *never* like her in the whole of a lifetime!"

And she had the distinct impression that, while the strains of the dreamy waltz tune filled her ears, and Peter guided her effortlessly, her employer, on the fringe of the floor, was frowning more noticeably than ever. But why she couldn't be at all certain.

Later, when she was sitting for the first time alone at the table, and resting rather aching feet in high-heeled silver sandals, he took the chair beside her and said:

"I should very much like the pleasure of dancing with you, Miss Waring, if your many importunate partners have not entirely worn you out."

She looked up into his dark eyes; they were strange and enigmatic, and regarding her with gravity as well.

"Thank you," she returned. "That is very kind of you, Dr. Fernandez" — and it was not intentional if her voice sounded a litle dry — "but is it permissible for an employer to dance with an employee at this sort of function?"

For a moment he looked straight down into her eyes, and she had the feeling that he was rebuking her in some strange way.

"Perfectly permissible, I should say. But you may not feel that you have the energy?"

"I have the energy!" And while Doña Beatriz watched them with narrowed eyes over the top of the shiny bald head of a short elderly man who was rushing her over the floor in a rather frenzied version of the tango, Lisa stood and melted into the arms of the man who was exactly a head and a half taller than she was, so that her golden hair strayed all over his white shirt front, and when he bent his head the tip of his square chin actually seemed to touch it, and nestle amongst the silken strands.

Lisa's heart was beating so wildly as she thought: "It would be a tango, this one and only dance I'll ever have with him! . . . And I'm not much good at dancing it, because I haven't had much experience!" that at first she really did muff her steps, and then she looked up at him helplessly. His eyes looked down into hers, and were so near to hers, that she gasped. . . . For there was nothing enigmatic in them now, and they seemed to glow in a way she had sometimes dreamed they might — if only she had an opportunity to know him better, and he to know her! If only their employer-employee relationship could be set aside for just a short while! . . .

Her lips fell a litle apart, opening softly, like the petals of a flower, and her eyes were suddenly clear and transparent as water. There was still a helpless look in them, too, and she knew it wasn't her imagination that he drew her closer into his arms.

"You dance beautifully," he said, "but you are almost too light for a human being! You are like thistledown!"

"I'm sure I'm much more solid than thistledown," she heard herself replying, and he smiled.

"You might be if you ate a great deal more, and someone took an enormous amount of care of you! I don't believe you are capable of taking a great deal of care of yourself," he declared rather musingly.

"I've done so for at least three years now," she told him, and he did not reply.

She gave herself up to the sheer bliss of dancing with him, and now that her moments of panic had passed, she realized that they danced beautifully together. Peter was a good dancer, and with him she had felt at her best, but Julio Fernandez made her conscious of surpassing herself. She supposed dreamily that it was because he was a member of a Latin race that his movements seemed to be fluid and almost boneless, so that she herself felt fluid and boneless, and it was just as if there was some fusion of their bodies that was not merely physical, but in part spiritual. In fact, it was *complete* fusion. . . . And it wasn't until the dance was over, and they were two separate entities again, that she realized how complete that temporary union had been.

But while it lasted the world about her ceased to exist, and her body floated in a haze of rapture, while her mind was almost dulled with the happiness of being where she was — in the arms of the man she loved!

The music was sensuous, and the rhythm like the regular throbbing of all her pulses. And when, having unconsciously closed her eyes, she opened them again to look up into the even-featured face above her, it struck her that that face was pale, and in the night-dark depths of the eyes something seemed to flame.

"I'm sorry," he said, and his words brought her down to earth, "about Gia. She should have maintained touch with you, and she should certainly have acknowleged the gift you sent her."

She sighed, and for a moment she couldn't answer, because talking was almost painful just then. And it seemed so unnecessary.

"It wasn't Gia's fault, I'm sure."

"Then are you suggesting——?"

She looked up at him with rather heavy eyes.

"I don't think Doña Beatriz was anxious for her to maintain touch with me!"

"But that's absurd!" he declared. "You are employed by me to have Gia's interests at heart. And naturally you would wonder about her."

"I have wondered," she admitted. "And I am still wondering whether you really want me to return with her to the villa? Because if not——"

"But of course I want you to return to the villa!" He frowned down at her. "Why should I not?"

"Because I think Doña Beatriz would prefer it otherwise!"

His frown dragged his black brows together until they almost overlapped.

"And is it the concern of Doña Beatriz——,"

"I think so," she said gently, the heavy eyes looking up directly into his. "Isn't it?"

All at once the music came to an end, and they stopped dancing so abruptly that, as he let her go rather suddenly, she lost her balance and found it necessary to make a little grab at him, but even so one of her high heels slipped, and her ankle twisted sharply. She caught her breath with the pain, and turned paler than she already was.

"You have hurt yourself? — your ankle?" he said, looking down at her in concern.

She shook her head, biting her lower lip.

"No, no, it's all right!"

He stood looking down at her, but she turned and walked firmly off the floor. He followed and, when she would have returned to their table, guided her away from it.

"I'll take you home," he said rather shortly.

But she looked up at him almost horrified.

"But of course you mustn't do that!" she said. "Take *me* home, when you're a guest at a party! ... And, in any case, Doña Beatriz ..."

"I think we'll leave Doña Beatriz out of things for the moment," he remarked, in the same terse voice. "You're looking rather white, and you're also very tired. We can leave a message for Miss

Tracey, and I'll make the necessary excuses to Señora Espinhaco. Have you a key to her flat, or is there someone who will admit you?"

"Juanita, Miss Tracey's maid, will be sitting up. She always insists on doing so, however late Miss Tracey is going to be! But I assure you there is no need . . ." feeling slightly sick even as she said so with the slight, nagging pain in her ankle.

His voice was rougher than she had ever known it.

"I think there is every need!" he said. "You have been doing more in this past fortnight than you are accustomed to doing — than it is wise to do at this season of the year in a place like Madrid. And now you have hurt your ankle. I am going to take you home."

"Very well," she answered, with a meekness that was quite unassumed, and she felt his arm about her, guiding her amongst the couples on the crowded floor.

"Get your wrap, and I will wait for you," he said, as soon as the brilliant restaurant doors had closed behind them, and they were outside in a spacious lobby.

"Very well," she returned, with even greater meekness than before.

CHAPTER FOURTEEN

ONCE IN HIS big white car, and being driven by him back to Miss Tracey's flat, she began to be absolutely certain that this was all part of a dream. When she had left the flat that evening to attend the Espinhaco birthday party the last person she expected to see amongst the guests was her employer, but he had been one of the guests, and now he was driving her home. Unless it was purely her imagination!

She really was very tired — even exhausted. It had been a stimulating, but rather wearing time that she had spent in Madrid, the heat had been intense, and tonight she had danced more than she had ever danced before in her life. There had been Ricardo Espinhaco who had claimed many of the dances, and who had only been persuaded to leave her side because his mother had plainly intimated that one or two of the other younger female guests were expecting some attention from him. And Peter had quite plainly resented Ricardo, and when she was not dancing with Ricardo she had danced with Peter.

It had all been a little too much!

She lay back against the luxuriously sprung seat and felt the cool night breeze coming in at the open windows, and sighed suddenly. All at once she was too utterly weary to do anything but relax, and even though it was her employer's car, and she was dragging him away not only from a party, but from the woman he was going to marry, she had to let some of the tension slide away from her, and sink back gratefully into the embrace of the dark crimson upholstery.

The breeze was particularly welcome after the slightly suffocating heat of the restaurant, following upon the concentrated heat of the day. She wasn't wearing a wrap; her pale shoulders gleamed in the darkness, and her skirts seemed to froth all over the place, and even to touch the regulation evening clothes of Dr. Fernandez. As she lay with her golden head against the back of the seat, staring out at the soft, smothering blackness that was Madrid at night, pierced by the splendor of the stars and the occasional lights that still shone like yellow lanterns in the quiet squares and avenues, she forgot for a moment where she was — until the doctor's hand reached out and touched her own.

"You are tired," he said, and his voice was much more like a caress. "You are really very tired, and the conquests you made tonight have exhausted you!" He paused. "Were they very satisfying conquests?"

She turned her head and looked at him.

"You mean because I danced with that young man Ricardo——?"

"Ricardo Espinhaco looked prepared to eat you at the moment of my arrival tonight, and there were others who looked capable of emulating his example!" His voice was all at once very dry. "And Peter Hamilton-Tracey is, of course, only waiting for you to be serious about him to be very serious about you!"

She stared at the dark, sleek shape of his head in the gloom of the car, and her whole body ached with a wave of longing for him that swept over her. The faint fragrance of his cigarette smoke, the scent of his shaving cream, both reached her in the gloom, and the combined effect of them set her trembling.

"Does a man wait until he is certain a woman is serious about him before he becomes serious about her?" she asked, with something of an effort.

He concentrated on his driving.

"If he is an Englishman I think he does! Or that is what my observation has taught me. If he is a Spaniard his impatience will not permit him to do that."

"And what," she asked, rather breathlessly, "would a Spaniard do?"

He went on frowning at the road ahead, the highway bathed in starlight, and overhung by plane tree shadows.

"If he was quite certain about his own feelings he might do many things," he replied, after what seemed to her an interminable pause; "but if he was not certain . . . well, then he would be more cautious!"

"I —see," she said, and her voice sounded both small and flat.

When they reached the block of flats where Miss Tracey lived he drew up before the ornate entrance. The flats towered above them, with their many balconies, and the gleaming white stone of which the block was constructed shone palely in the starlight. It was no paler than Lisa's small, tired face when he helped her from the car.

Instead of putting her into the lift, as she had expected, and allowing her to make her own way alone up to the flat, he followed her when the gilded doors swung open, and it was he who pressed the button that sent them slowly whirring skywards. Lisa began:

"There is really no need for you to come up with me . . ."

He stood very close to her in the narrow, enclosed space, and in the soft light that glowed above their heads he still seemed to want to study her. He made no reply to her half-hearted protest that she could have found her way up alone, and when the lift stopped with a click, and then the gates closed behind them, he accompanied her along the corridor to the white-painted door that bore the number of Miss Tracey's flat. Lisa put out her hand to depress the bell, but he stopped her suddenly.

"You will go straight to bed?" he said. "And this Juanita of Miss Tracey's — will she bring you some hot milk, or some sort of soothing drink?"

"I don't need a soothing drink," she began to assure him, but the look on his face told her that was no good at all, and she promised rather hurriedly: "I will ask Juanita to make me a cup of tea. She knows I love tea."

He smiled.

"You English and your tea!"

"Or there is really no reason why I shouldn't make it myself. Poor Juanita has sat up long enough. . . ."

"If you threaten to do that," he said, "I will come in and insist on making it for you!"

All at once she thought wildly:

"If only I had the courage to ask him in, and get Juanita to provide refreshments for us both! If only I had the courage to make tea for us both! He probably wouldn't drink it, but if I suggested it he might come in. . . ."

Something of what she was thinking must have been transmitted to him, or something at any rate flashed between them — some desire on her part to delay him, some disinclination on his to depart hurriedly — for all at once he said:

"I don't like leaving you like this."

And then, as she looked up at him in surprise, her large eyes as soft and limpid as a child's in the dim golden light of the corridor, her soft lips once more falling a little apart, he made an abrupt movement and swept her into his arms, and obeying a wild impulse she reached out and clutched at him, and for moments that for her were quite delirious she was strained up against him, and his mouth came down and closed upon her mouth, and the light in the corridor revolved like a shining lamp.

His lips were hard, and sweet, and masculine, as she had always known they would be. . . . The fire that she had always suspected dwelt in him flashed like a living thing to the surface, and all at once his lips were burning hers, and he said something rapidly in Spanish that passed her by altogether, although she knew that they were words that surprised himself as much as they would have surprised her if she could have understood them. Then she did understand that he was saying her name over and over again, wonderingly, as if it delighted him:

"Lisa! . . . Little Lisa! . . . *Querida!* . . ."

His lips pressed her eyelids, her white forehead, the gold tendrils of her hair that rested on her forehead; and then for another brief period of time that simply wasn't time at all, but utter bliss, she surrendered her mouth to him again. When he let her go at last she was no longer pale, but her eyes looked dazed, and because she was quite sure this was something he would regret the very moment he left her she put out a hand and pressed desperately at the door bell.

They heard Juanita's footsteps ponderously approaching the door, and she said in what she tried frantically to make a normal voice:

"You must let me know when you — you want me to return to the villa. When you want me to take over Gia again. . . ."

As the door opened, and Juanita looked out at them, he answered:

"Very well, I will." His voice sounded cool and almost ordinary. "And in the meantime you must go straight to bed. Juanita," suavely addressing the servant, "see to it that Miss Waring goes straight to bed, will you . . . ?"

CHAPTER FIFTEEN

THE next morning Lisa faced the problem of what she had to do in the immediate future, and it was really no problem at all, because she had worked it all out in the night. She had scarcely slept at all, in spite of her physical weariness when she lay down, and she knew it was because her mind had been so alert, and her sense so awakened that sleep was an unreasonable thing to expect under the circumstances.

But in the golden light of morning she knew what she had to do. She had to see Julio Fernandez at once and ask him whether he would allow her to return to the coast with Gia without delay, because otherwise she couldn't remain in Spain. She certainly couldn't stay on in Madrid living this butterfly life that Miss Tracey had thought would provide her with a welcome interlude — which it certainly had done. But to go on living it, even though Miss Tracey was so kind, and so extraordinarily generous, would be impossible. For one thing it would be impossible because she couldn't go on taking advantage of Miss Tracey's kindness, and for another, now that she knew that she had some sort of physical attraction for Dr. Fernandez, the sooner she got away from him the better; and she had promised to take charge of his daughter until she went to school. It would only be until the autumn, and the autumn was not so very far away now, and after that — after that she would go home.

She bit her lip as she started to go through her wardrobe and pack some of her things. She was confident that the doctor would let her go back at once with Gia, for after last night he wouldn't want the danger of running into her constantly at social affairs — affairs given by his own particular friends, who would certainly look upon it as odd if he repeated last night's performance and disappeared before the party was over with his small daughter's governess, apparently for the pleasure of seeing her home!

For who would believe that it was because he had been concerned about her that he had taken her home? And it was his concern that had led to that — those blissful moments outside the closed door of Miss Tracey's flat, which Lisa at least would never forget, because that sort of experience was hardly likely to come her way again. She had little or no conceit, and although Ricardo had succumbed to her English type of looks, and Peter was displaying every symptom of being willing to fall in love with her, Dr. Fernandez was quite unlike either of these two men — *and he simply was not the type of man to fall for his daughter's governess!*

A sudden, overwhelming urge to kiss an attractive girl was one thing, but anything more serious would never enter his head. She was so certain of that she felt a little sick as she went on with her packing.

And even if it did enter his head, there was Doña Beatriz . . . Doña Beatriz, who was the right type of woman for him, and who planned to marry him. It was quite obvious that all their friends were of the same mind about that.

Therefore it was doubly important that she should get away at once, back to a suitable obscurity.

When Aunt Grizel came into her room, wearing the usual bathrobe, she looked surprised to see her young guest up so early.

"My dear, you are energetic!" she declared. Then she looked at the slowly filling suitcase, but said nothing about it. "What happened last night?" she asked. "Juanita says that Dr. Fernandez brought you home, and that you looked very tired. Was the evening too much for you?"

"No, but I twisted my ankle while dancing, and Dr. Fernandez was kind enough to offer to run me back here." She looked a little guiltily at her hostess. "I hope it wasn't rude disappearing like that, and that you didn't mind? That Señora Espinhaco didn't mind? Dr. Fernandez said he would leave a message explaining why we had gone."

"Well, he didn't do so, my dear — but it didn't matter. I think most people saw the two of you depart, and Doña Beatriz certainly saw you go!" She paused. "Ricardo looked a bit upset after you had gone, and I don't think Peter was pleased, but Dr. Fernandez is not the type to consider small fry like that. He obviously thought you needed bed, so he brought you home." Another pause. "How is the ankle this morning?"

"Better." Lisa looked down at it as if she had forgotten it altogether ."Much better."

"And why are you up so early?"

Suddenly Lisa decided she had better explain, and she did so.

"I feel I ought to go back. That I've had a long enough holiday. And really," looking almost apologetically at the older woman who was watching her with very shrewd eyes, "it has been a wonderful change, and you've been so terribly good to me. But I couldn't go on accepting your hospitality like this, and — and I don't feel Madrid is the sort of place for me to remain in. . . ."

"Did Dr. Fernandez ask you to return to the coast last night?"

"No, but I feel I ought to. You see, he insists on paying my salary, and I can't receive a salary and do nothing for it. . . ."

"I suppose not," Miss Tracey murmured, staring down at the satin bed-cover while she sat perched on the side of the bed.

"And that's why I've made up my mind to go and see him today and— and ask if I can take Gia back at once. After all, it can't be good for a child in this hot weather in Madrid, and she does need the sea air. And I want to take her back."

Miss Tracey rose and stood facing her.

"You want to get away from Madrid because you'd feel happier if you didn't bump into your employer at parties in the way you did last night, isn't that it?" she said very gently.

Lisa nodded silently, and Miss Tracey sighed.

"Poor child!" she exclaimed. "I hoped you might fall for Peter in time, or some other nice young man I might produce for you. But it seems I was a little late."

Lisa swallowed.

"Yes; I'm afraid you were a little late."

"In that case," the older woman said, walking to the window and staring out at the brightness of early morning Madrid, "I think you're wise to want to get away. And as soon as you can be freed I would go home to England."

"I will," Lisa replied, as if she was making her a solemn promise.

Miss Tracey returned to her and patted her bright hair.

"Never mind, child, you're young, and——" She sighed again, and then put sentiment away from her. "You know where the doctor lives? He has a very sumptuous flat in what was once a very fine town house, but I imagine he lives by his appointment book. Oughtn't you to telephone and make certain he is free? His consulting rooms are not in the same building as his flat, but his secretary could tell you what he is likely to be doing."

"No, I think I'll go straight to his flat," Lisa said, although she wasn't quite sure why she arrived at that decision. It wasn't curiosity to see the doctor's flat. "It's early, and I should think I'll almost certainly find him there."

"And you won't telephone?"

"No—no, I won't telephone."

It was odd, she thought later, how a decision of that sort could affect the whole of one's future life. If she had telephoned Julio's secretary, or even telephoned him at his flat, she probably wouldn't have run into Doña Beatriz when she arrived there, and found her in sole occupation of the luxuriously-furnished sitting-room that overlooked one of Madrid's most leafy avenues.

Doña Beatriz was going round the room rearranging the flowers in the vases, and although it was so early in the day, and she herself couldn't have been very early to bed the previous night, she was looking almost aggressively fresh and immaculate in a dove-grey silk suit with touches of white, and extremely high-heeled, hand-made shoes that made her elegant, Spanish woman's feet look at least a couple of sizes smaller and more shapely than they actually were.

"Good morning, Miss Waring!" she greeted Lisa, when a deferential manservant had shown her into the sitting-room. "This is rather early for a call on your employer, isn't it? — And, incidentally, he's a very busy man, which perhaps you didn't know, and doesn't normally receive anyone at this hour!"

Her voice was cold as the drip of ice, and she was holding a long-stemmed scarlet rose in her hand. As she spoke her beringed fingers, with their crimson nails, caressed the petals of the rose with deliberately graceful movements.

"I'm sorry," Lisa replied. "I was aware that Dr. Fernandez is a busy man, but I particularly wanted to see him."

"That doesn't surprise me so very much," Doña Beatriz drawled. She surveyed the English girl, in her simple linen outfit, with openly hostile eyes. "My dear Miss Waring, you may not realize it, but you are almost painfully transparent. From the very beginning it has been clear to me that as a governess you left quite a lot to be desired, but although Dr. Fernandez is an unusually attractive man, even I didn't suspect that you might become a menace to his reputation! Miss Waring!" She moved nearer to her, still caressing the rose. "Last night you caused everyone to look surprised when you seized upon an unexpected meeting to get him to take you away from a private party at an unusually early hour, and as he did not return to that party you can imagine what his friends thought? And what *I* would have thought if I didn't know him a little better than you do!"

Lisa felt herself turning cold, and she stammered slightly.

"I'm afraid I don't know what you mean!"

"Don't you?" Doña Beatriz looked contemptuous. "I think you do. But let me tell you one thing. Dr. Fernandez and I are going to marry very soon now — most of the details are arranged, although we have not yet informed our friends — and I do not like to see a young girl like you making an exhibition of herself because of him. Perhaps it is not your fault — as I have said, the doctor is attractive, and you *are* young! — but I happen to know that you have been causing him embarrassment for several weeks now, and that is the reason why he appealed to me to do something to help him before the embarrassment got too acute. He asked me to take Gia away, and I decided to bring her here to Madrid — at a certain amount of inconvenience to myself, I might add."

"But I don't understand what you are talking about!" Lisa got out in a rush. She was as white as a sheet, and her pulses were thundering with shock. "You say that I have caused Dr. Fernandez embarrassment?"

"Rather a lot of embarrassment, I'm afraid," Doña Beatriz answered smoothly. "Perhaps you don't realize it, but to a nice man the sight of a girl in tears, suffering from pretended shock after stupidly interfering with a half-savage dog, and openly pleading with her every look to be taken into his arms and comforted, is rather *more* than embarrassing! And last night it was a twisted ankle! . . . I have no doubt there have been other occasions, possibly a little more ingeniously thought out. So can you wonder at it that Dr. Fernandez would have been most unlikely to see you this morning, even if he had been here?"

Lisa was now quite white even to the lips, and her eyes looked like the eyes of an injured creature.

"I — don't know how you can say such things!" she gasped. "I have never — *never!* — embarrassed Dr. Fernandez! It was true I——" she remembered the night before, and turned crimson instead of white — "I was upset when the dog attacked me, but I didn't want any comfort. Oh!" She put up a hand and touched her mouth, like someone too lacerated to be conscious of what she was doing. "You say that Dr. Fernandez complained about me? And that he asked you to take Gia away?"

"Well, my dear, he didn't complain about you in so many words, but I could sense his embarrassment. "I know that he felt rather helpless, because he had engaged you, and you hadn't turned out to be quite what he expected. The first little shock was discovering you on the beach with that English boy friend of yours, Peter Hamilton-Tracey, and after that he hardly felt he could trust you. But I think he would have been prepared to keep you on if — well, if he hadn't begun to suspect that your interest in the Hamilton-Tracey youth was being transferred to himself! After that he became concerned."

"I see," Lisa said. Dully she half turned away, and then she turned back again. "Last night," she managed, looking Doña Beatriz fully in the eyes, "Dr. Fernandez told me that he wanted me to return to the villa with Gia as soon as you were ready to part with her. But that, I suppose, is not any longer true?"

"I'm afraid not," Doña Beatriz returned, on the same note of complacence. "As a matter of fact, our plans for Gia are now fully decided upon, and she is not returning to the villa. She is going to stay with friends of mine for a week or two — friends who have young people of her own age, and who also have a villa beside the sea, and where she will be very happy and content. At least, until she goes to school."

"And you have also decided upon her school?" Lisa asked, in a choked voice.

Doña Beatriz nodded.

"I think so. And it will be in England," she added. "Her mother was partly English — although perhaps you didn't know that?"

"Yes, I did," Lisa admitted.

"And she was *very* beautiful!" the Spanish woman informed her with emphasis. "Dr. Fernandez was very upset by her death — so upset that any lack of interest in his daughter you might have suspected was entirely due to the shock he received when the mother died. Some men take these things badly, especially when a birth involves the loss of a far more precious life."

"Yes, I — see!" Lisa heard herself saying mechanically, and realized that that was what she had always suspected. Julio Fernandez had loved once, and deeply — and not even Doña Beatriz was ever likely to arouse that love again!

It was the one thing she ought to be able to feel sympathy with Doña Beatriz over.

But she didn't feel sympathy with her. She was too stunned and disturbed to feel sympathy with anyone just then.

She turned away.

"I'm sorry I've troubled you this morning," she said, in an unnaturally controlled voice. "I'll go now."

Doña Beatriz followed her, still holding the single scarlet rose, to the door.

"I think you are taking this very sensibly," she said. "And it will be easier if you go home to England without much more delay. After all, there must be many more interests for you in your own country. I'll tell Dr. Fernandez you took the decision to go home yourself."

"Yes, please do that," Lisa answered, but whatever decision she now took it was too late to undo the final humiliation she had brought upon herself as a result of the night before. He had taken her in his arms to comfort her, no doubt because he suspected she badly needed that comfort — and she had let him!

She felt almost blind and deaf with humiliation as she found her way out into the strong sunlight. She felt that Madrid was a sun-soaked trap that had done something to her that could never be undone.

CHAPTER SIXTEEN

MISS TRACEY took one look at her when she arrived back at the flat, and decided that it would be wisest not to ask any questions. But when Lisa announced that she wanted to go home at once she not only looked her concern, but expressed it.

"But, my dear child, you can't do that!" she said. "If by 'going home' you mean going home to England, you can't do it as suddenly as all this!"

"I can," Lisa answered. "And I must go!" she added.

Aunt Grizel's expression became rather hopeless.

"I feel it's no concern of mine, so I'm not going to probe into your reasons," she told the girl; "but I've grown very fond of you, and I've got your welfare at heart. I happen to know you've got very few friends in England, so what will you do when you get there? You can't exist without money, and you can't expect to walk back into a job immediately!"

"I'll find a job very quickly," Lisa tried to convince her, in a voice from which all life had gone. "With children, of course," she added. "There are always children to be looked after."

"Other people's children!" Miss Tracey commented. "It's about time, my dear, you started to possess children of your own!"

Then as she saw how the girl winced as if something had wounded her internally she went to her and took her by her slender shoulders and held them firmly.

"Look, child, I said I wasn't going to probe — and I won't if you simply can't bear the idea of my doing so. But won't you tell me one thing? Did you see Dr. Fernandez this morning?

"No," Lisa barely whispered.

"You saw someone?"

"I saw Doña Beatriz!"

"Oh!" Aunt Grizel exclaimed. She peered into Lisa's face. "Doña Beatriz said, or did, something to upset you?"

Lisa shook her head dumbly, and then admitted:

"There is no longer any need for me to look after Gia. Other plans have been made for her, and — and Doña Beatriz is going to marry Dr. Fernandez — soon!"

"I see," Miss Tracey said, and released Lisa's shoulders and walked away from her. When she returned she tried to make her voice and her look severely practical. "In that case, perhaps it's as well that you should go home fairly soon — but I must say I don't understand why you should be dismissed like this. Doña Beatriz is not Dr. Fernandez' wife yet, and there may be some mistake. Perhaps if *I* spoke to Dr. Fernandez himself on the telephone——"

"No, no!" Lisa cried, almost hysterically, at once, and Aunt Grizel felt suddenly very much enlightened.

"Very well, my dear, but presumably you'll have to see him before you leave?"

"I won't see him!" with a tightening of the lips that was quite unlike the usual gentle Lisa. "I'll never see him again!"

And she meant it. Once away from Spain she would do her utmost — and only she knew how difficult that would be! — to put him not only out of her life but out of her thoughts, for he had behaved in a way she would never have believed of him. He had talked about her to another woman—the woman he was to marry, admittedly, but a woman who was hostile to Lisa. He had admitted that the English girl embarrassed him,

172

although how, or in what way, she had embarrassed him she couldn't think. Only last night she hadn't really thought it wise that they should leave the party together — not without saying a word of farewell to either their host or hostess, and she had reminded him that Doña Beatriz might not like it. But he had said quite curtly that they would leave Doña Beatriz out of it. And not very long afterwards he had kissed her as if he had wanted to do that for a long time!

All night she had lain awake feeling the touch of his lips. The way they had closed almost hungrily over her mouth, and the manner in which he had murmured her name, over and over again, and sought to keep her in his arms, had not at the time seemed a very clear indication that the whole episode was one-sided, and that it was she who had tempted him by some unwary glance. He might be sorry for her — perhaps he was — but he didn't have to take pity on her to that extent.

After all, she had not been without admirers all the evening! She had not been exactly a wallflower at the party! . . .

But now she was too sick at heart to care much why he had behaved as he had. She only knew that from now on even the thought of his name would cover her in humiliation, and it was a humiliation that felt like dust and ashes in her mouth. She had never known one could feel as despised and rejected as this.

"Listen to me, Lisa," Aunt Grizel was saying. "If you go home to England where will you stay? Have you *any* friends you can go to?"

Lisa didn't bother to answer the last part of the question.

"I'll find myself a room," she said. "I'll go to an hotel for a night or two, and then look for a room. Or maybe I'll be lucky and get something to do immediately."

"You don't want to go rushing into the first job that falls vacant. Listen, Lisa," she insisted again, "I have a little cottage in Cornwall that is empty at the moment but there is a woman who looks after it for me, and she'll look after you. I want you to go there and stay there until you can find something you like, or something you *feel* you will like to do. But please don't rush into anything! I'm terribly fond of you, Lisa," she sounded just a trifle wistful, "and I'd hoped you might stay with me longer, but I realize you can't do that. I don't quite know why, but you've got to get away. And that being so will you go to Tressida Cottage?"

"Tressida Cottage?" Lisa echoed, a little stupidly.

"Yes; it's right on the edge of the cliffs, and very attractive. No one will disturb you, and my woman will cook for you, and do anything else for you you want. And if you can bear it you can have the place right through the winter. Though it can be lonely in the winter months . . ." she ended doubtfully.

Lisa suddenly made up her mind.

"Tressida Cottage?" she repeated. "I'll go there!" Her face brightened suddenly at the thought of getting away from everything and everyone connected with the past few months, and then it suddenly struck her how ungrateful she was appearing, and she implored Miss Tracey to believe that she would have stayed with her just a little longer if she could, but she couldn't. "You've been so kind," she said, "so terribly kind! And it's been a wonderful fortnight! Until last night I — I was enjoying it."

"Were you?" Miss Tracey murmured, but she sounded as if she needed convincing. "Well, I don't know how Peter's going to take your sudden vanishing. . . . And what am I to say to Dr. Fernandez if he comes here?"

"Nothing," Lisa replied immediately, but with great insistence. "Just tell him I had to go!"

"And you don't think it might be fair to let him know why — or in part why — you had to go?"

"No, no!" Lisa sounded horrified. "Tell him nothing, please! Just — ask him to give my love to Gia!"

She thought about Gia all the way to England, and curiously enough she felt that Gia would be as unhappy over this business as she was herself. Gia had grown fond of her, Gia had trusted her, and now she was disappearing out of Gia's life as she was out of Gia's father's. In the case of the child the disappearance might come a little hard, but the father would feel nothing but relief!

Lisa's cheeks burned so painfully that the color seemed to scorch her skin every time she remembered how much she had embarrassed him, and how proportionately strong his relief would be when he knew that he was never likely to be embarrassed again in the same way!

When she reached England the grey skies and the chill wind seemed to indicate that summer had already departed, and all the way down to Cornwall the impression grew stronger and stronger. There were powerful seas, and the little white cottage was perched rather perilously near to the edge of the cliffs that overlooked the empty beach. It was a cottage that reminded her of a blind eye — or, rather, two blind eyes, which were the windows of the downstairs rooms, one on either side of a narrow hall — looking hopelessly to see if someone wouldn't come and occupy it, and bring back the warmth of human company.

Lisa felt that she was hardly the human company the cottage craved when the taxi-man deposited her suitcase in the road a dozen or so yards from the gate of the cottage itself. There was no actual road leading up to the gate of the cottage, and the taxi-man seemed anxious not to risk his cab too near to the edge of the cliffs.

"Sorry, miss, but I don't mind carrying the case in for you," he said. When they reached the green-painted front door he asked for the key. "Bit lonely for a young woman like you," he remarked, when he had swung open the door, "but I expect you like the sea?"

The inference was that he wasn't very fond of it himself, and remembering the variegated seas that had crashed silkily on the beach of the Costa Brava, and the villa with its garden — which she would never see again! — ablaze beside those perenially sun-kissed waters, and the rose-red and emerald-green rocks to which she and Gia had so frequently clung like limpets in sun-suits, Lisa felt all at once quite appalled to be where she was. Not that she hadn't once spent a very happy holiday in Cornwall, and admired it at the time. But Cornwall was not — the Costa Brava!

And the Costa Brava was not Madrid!

"Yes, I'm very fond of the sea," she admitted, and then tipped the man with a generosity that surprised him, and walked into the stone-flagged kitchen. Mrs. Pendennis had left a bottle of milk for her in the larder, a fresh loaf in the bread-bin, a quarter of tea beside the kettle that was filled and ready to plug in to the electric point, and a note which explained that her youngest had had toothache, and that she had had to get him to the dentist, which meant that she would not put in an appearance until the following day. But the beds in both bedrooms were aired, and if Lisa switched on the immersion heater she would be able to have a bath.

Lisa looked around the empty, cold litle kitchen, and wondered whether she could summon up the energy to have a bath. Her journey from Spain seemed to have exhausted her, mentally as well

176

as physically, and all she craved was oblivion, and the comfort of clean sheets. And perhaps in the morning a touch of sun would restore some of the normality that seemed to have departed from her, and give her more courage to face the future.

But in the night the wind grew stronger, and by morning the sea wasn't merely pounding the beach, it was thundering against the very walls of the cottage — or so it seemed. Rain drove against the windows, rain and spray and great lumps of spume like soapsuds.

Lisa stayed inside all morning, and then put on a mackintosh and fought her way through the gale to the nearest tiny store where she could obtain supplies, and there learned that Mrs. Pendennis's youngest had had a bad time at the dentist's, and that it was unlikely she would put in an appearance that day. The woman in the shop seemed sympathetic to learn that Lisa was quite alone, and expressed the opinion that the storm would get worse.

"We get 'em in these parts!" she remarked ominously.

They certainly "got 'em" before nightfall, and by nightfall Lisa's nerves were beginning to be worn with the constant shrieking of the wind, and the battering of the sea against the cliff which supported the cottage. She lighted a fire in the sitting-room grate and sat by it, trying to lose herself in one of the books left behind by Miss Tracey, and at nine o'clock she made herself a hot drink and put a hot-water bottle in her bed. It was still summer, it was true, but the storm made it very cold — unless it was she who felt cold and unhappy and desperate as she went lifelessly about these attempts to minister to her own comfort.

She thought of herself doing this sort of thing throughout the winter, sheltering from reality in Miss Tracey's cottage, seeing no one save Mrs.

Pendennis and the woman at the shop, and concerned only with keeping her little larder well stocked.

While far away in Madrid! . . .

She went to bed with the hot-water bottle, and perhaps because it really was a comfort she slept well that night — deep and dreamlessly, in spite of the storm that raged without. And in the morning, when she sat up in bed and looked from the tiny window, the storm had abated, and the sun was shining brilliantly, and everything was deliciously green and gold and blue.

A green and gold and blue world! . . . Just a little like the Costa Brava!

She fairly sprang from her bed, and without waiting to make herself any breakfast, or even tea, washed and dressed and went outside and stood in a state of bemused admiration in the tiny front garden. From the garden a path led down to the beach, but it was not an easy path, and the rocks amongst which it meandered were sharp as dragon's teeth, grey as roof slates that had been touched by hoar-frost, and slippery with receding moisture that was being slowly drawn up into the atmosphere by the warmth of the sun.

And the sun was warm this morning — warm and benevolent, and inclined to act as a false boost to morale. Nothing, in that sunlight, could strike one as quite as bad as it actually was, and Lisa wanted to feel more of it on her body, striking down on to her uncovered head, seeping into every pore of her mental fibre like a lovely, soothing sedative. The garden was partly in shadow because of the walls of the house, so she adventured towards the edge of the cliff, and then started to descend the cliff path.

She wore rubber-soled sandals, and they slithered on the rocks. Half-way down she began to feel uncertain of herself, and when she looked upwards at the wall of cliff behind her her uncertainty seemed to spread, because the tiny cottage now seemed almost inaccessible, and the beach was still a considerable distance below her.

She never had had a very good head for heights, and she realized now that it would have been wiser if she had waited for that early-morning cup of tea. She had lived on practically nothing the day before, having no appetite — and what interest was there in preparing meals when there was only yourself? — and she felt a little hollow inside. In fact, quite disturbingly hollow.

When she looked downwards her head swam. When she looked upwards she wanted to crouch down and cling to the jagged, needle-pointed rocks that were all about her.

And below her the sea swirled, dazzling her, continuing to bemuse her with its shimmer, and the long call of gulls reminded her that they were the only other living creatures near her.

A sense of panic shook her. She'd have to try and get back *up* the cliff! She didn't think she could go on down!

And then a voice not very far away ordered her to remain where she was. She looked round upwards, and saw that someone was making his or her way to her — at that distance, and with the blinding light of the sun in her eyes, she couldn't see whether it was a man or a woman. But when the figure came nearer the voice was unmistakably masculine, and it ordered her more peremptorily not to move. Not to take a single step either backwards or forwards.

"I'll be with you in a minute!" the calm voice said, and this time Lisa's heart turned over, and her knees started to tremble, because it wasn't just an ordinary English voice. . . . There was a kind of accent to it — an accent she would never forget!

The next moment he landed on the rock beside her, and he looked extraordinarily English in a tweed suit that looked as if it had been made by an English tailor, and a carelessly flowing tie that was caught by the breeze and almost whipped into her face when he was within a foot of her. Then she looked up into a dark, rather shut-in face that could never be taken as purely English, and into eyes that had often reminded her of midnight pools, because they were so inscrutable. Only now the eyes were blazing with concern, although the mouth was compressed, and the strong chin looked rigid. His black hair shone in the sunlight.

"Did you lose your nerve?"

His voice was quiet, almost casual, and as she answered she tore at her lower lip in a way that caused a tiny drop of blood to spurt.

"I must have done. I—I'm not very good at heights!"

"But you're all right now."

His arm was round her, and he was holding her tight, and for the moment her amazement was drowned in the miracle of his appearance, and although she didn't recognize her own reaction she clung to him, and he could feel how she trembled as she did so.

"How did you get here?" she asked, after what seemed to her an eternity of blissfully relieved silence.

"It doesn't matter now," he answered. "Let's get back to the top of the cliff. And remember there's nothing to be afraid of, because I'm with you and I won't let you fall. Just give me your hand. . . . ."

She gave it to him, and he looked down deep into her eyes.

"You came down alone, but you're going back with me! It's as simple as that, *querida*! Do you understand?"

With her free hand she thrust back an end of her fair hair that the wind had whipped into her eyes, and then he could see that the grey eyes were glistening like the restless surface of the sea. They were clear, transparent, utterly trusting eyes.

"Yes," she answered, "I understand."

CHAPTER SEVENTEEN

ONCE SAFELY back on the top of the cliff he refused to allow her to look down, but led her to a wooden bench near the front door of the cottage, and when she sank down on it sat down beside her.

"And what would have happened, I wonder," he asked, in a voice such as she had never heard from him before, "if I hadn't been here?"

Lisa looked up into eyes that seemed to be haunted by his concern, and although she was still pale from her experience, he was several degrees paler. It was a pallor resulting from inner dread, from a horrifying conviction that if he hadn't been on the spot to prevent it she might have made some unwary move, or lost her nerve altogether down there on those needle-pointed rocks. And at the picture the thought conjured up his voice shook uncontrollably.

"Lisa, *why* did you do this thing to me?" he demanded hoarsely.

"Why?" As she looked at him she knew without a shadow of doubt that she had done something to him over the past few years that had transformed him so far as she was concerned, but remembering why she had had to do that thing — and her own so very recent sufferings! — she pretended that she didn't understand. "I don't know what you mean. What have I done to you?"

He looked at her almost sadly, the lustrous eyes filled with reproach.

"You left Madrid without even a word to me. Without even a word for Gia! If it hadn't been for Miss Tracey I wouldn't have known where to find you, or where to look for you."

"Was there any reason why you had to find me?" The chill in her voice widened his eyes still further, and she rushed on: "I simply do not understand why you are here, Dr. Fernandez! — why you came all this way in pursuit of me, apparently! And, in any case, Miss Tracey had no real right to let you know where I am. She promised——"

"She promised," he took the words out of her mouth, gently, "not to volunteer where you were to be found, but not to refuse information if it was asked for. And naturally she knew it would be asked for, as you must have done. Lisa!" He reached forth a hand and covered both of hers, which were clinging to one another almost desperately in her lap. "Oh, *querida*, I still want to know why you thought I had to be made to suffer tortures of anxiety about you, particularly when Miss Tracey told me how upset you were! She is upset, too, because she has grown fond of you, and Gia is very fond of you. While I——"

"You?" she said, lifting her eyes from the brown, slim hand that was giving back life and warmth to her fingers, and searching his face almost hopefully for an instant. Then her lower lip trembled, and she had to bite it hard to steady it, and she managed: "You, Dr. Fernandez, have been embarrassed by me, and I thought you would be very grateful if I removed the embarrassment. I removed it as far away as I could. I came here. . . ."

"Yes, but that is what I do not understand! And why do you talk of embarrassment?"

Suddenly she snatched away her hands, and covered her eyes with them.

"Please!" she begged, in a muffled voice. "When I'm with you I always seem to behave in a way I shouldn't! There was the night when my foot caught in the jetty, and then you had to treat a graze on my arm, and I — I was stupid! Then

183

at the Espinhaco's party I twisted my ankle, and I took you away from the party! . . ."

The tears were trickling down her cheeks, and she tried to conceal them from him with her fingers, but he took the fingers back into his own warm clasp and removed them firmly and looked at her.

"Even if all this is right, why do you catalogue these things?" he asked. "And there is one thing you have forgotten. On the night of the Espinhaco's party you allowed me to kiss you!"

"Y-yes!"

Her eyes swimming in tears, she looked at him pleadingly. Whether she was pleading for another kiss, or apologizing for her weakness on the night of the Espinhaco party, they were neither of them ever afterwards quite certain, but he did know that he couldn't bear the sight of the pathetically quivering lower lip any longer, and she knew that if his arms hadn't closed round her she would have hurled herself into them.

He held her with a mixture of fierceness and tenderness.

"My darling," he said softly, into her hair, "my sweet and most precious darling! Oh, Lisa, I love you so much, and you must have known! — you *must* have known! Right from the beginning I knew you were a challenge to me, but I've grown into a routine way of life that didn't want anything to do with challenges, and I refused to accept it. But for weeks now I've known that I could never let you go out of my life! . . ."

"But — but you're going to marry Doña Beatriz," she stammered feebly into his neck.

"Am I ?" He sounded interested. "That is news to me, my dear one! How did you hear it, and when?"

Lisa burrowed deeper into his neck. If it wasn't true it seemed pointless to involve Doña Beatriz at this stage. But on the other hand . . .

But he was insistent now that he began to get an inkling of why she had run away.

"*Where* did you hear it, and *when*?" he persisted, you've got to tell me. Because if I am already pledged to another woman, how can I ask you to marry me?"

"M-marry you?"

He looked deep into her eyes, tilting up her chin.

"I want you for my wife more than anything in this world," he told her almost solemnly, "and if you hadn't run away when you did I was coming to tell you so that very same night! I bought a mass of scarlet roses to send to you that morning after the dance, but somehow I hadn't the courage. . . . Not until I was absolutely sure that you loved me, too. Oh, Lisa, my darling——"

"Scarlet roses!" she gasped, sitting upright in his arms. Suddenly she knew that she had seen those scarlet roses and one of them had been emphasizing the whiteness of Doña Beatriz's hand on that morning when she called at Juilo's flat! And now she wondered, had Doña Beatriz known for whom those roses had been originally intended? Suddenly she sank back against him. "Scarlet roses!" she whispered.

He held her strongly.

"You must tell me all there is to be told," he insisted with a note of sternness in his voice, "You came to my flat on that last morning in Madrid, didn't you?"

"How do you know?"

"Never mind how I know. But you saw Beatriz, didn't you?"

"I — she was there, yes."

"And what did she say to you?"

"She——" Helplessly she hid her face again. "Oh, never mind, now! So long as you are not going to marry her!"

"I do mind, and I am not going to marry her! Lisa," forcing her face into the open again, "you have suffered badly, and I have suffered badly, and I must know the reason. What did Beatriz say to you, apart from inventing a story about marrying me?"

"And there never has been any truth in it? You never did intend to marry her, I mean? Although she practically ran your house and your daughter?"

"No, never — and I can explain these other accusations later. But for the moment we shall stick to the point, *and what did Beatrice say?*"

"She — she said that I was running after you, and that I embarrassed you! That you had confessed to her how much I embarrassed you, and that you had appealed to her to take Gia away, so that you could get rid of me! Oh, Julio," she told him, her whole face quivering as well as her voice, "it was horrible!"

"It was very horrible!" he agreed. He rested his face against her hair, and she felt as if his arms were straining her to him protectively. "But although it was almost criminal, why did you believe her? Have I ever given you reason to believe that I would discuss you with another woman? Am I the type of man, do you think, who would do that? Especially when you must have known that for me you had a charm that was more powerful than anything that had entered my life!"

"But I didn't know!" she told him. "Julio, I didn't know! I thought you were kind. . . . I thought perhaps you liked me sometimes, but I didn't think you were the sort of man who——"

"Would look for the one perfect rose in the garden?"

She lifted her head and gazed into his eyes. His were black and lustrous, and they seemed to possess her. Hers started to glow.

"Am I — I that to you?" she asked.

"You are! And what am I to you?"

Suddenly courage came to her, shyness vanished, and she lifted her arms and wound them round his neck. Her eyes weren't merely transparent now, they were abject, adoring.

"You are the only man I could ever love in the whole of my lifetime! In a dozen lifetimes! You are the reason why I wished I had the courage to throw myself into the sea when I was part-way down the cliff just now, and why I couldn't even start to make any plans for the future. I hadn't any future without you, and without Gia. I love you both, but I love you more than life!"

"Querida!" The word was jerked out of him as if it was part of a long-suppressed inner turmoil, and then once again his lips came down upon hers, and she savored the bliss of surrendering to a man who would possess her always, and completely. There would never be any half measures between them — only *utter* belonging, and desire that was like a flame. Her whole body trembled with it, and his arms tightened to give her the final shred of conviction she needed that this was something far more vital than the dreams she had indulged in, and her mouth was like a scarlet flower when at last he lifted his head. He looked down at it broodingly. "Why does a man love one woman, and one only?" he wanted to know. "Why is she so important to him that without her he never really comes alive?"

She put up a hand and touched his face.

"But — but it is possible to love more than once, isn't it?"

"Not as I love you!" His olive skin darkened, and for the first time it was really borne in on her that he was no Englishman, but a Spaniard who could become fiercely jealous if the cause was provided — perhaps if it was not provided!

"Lisa, if you think that it is possible to love more than once——"

"I don't — *I* don't!" she assured him immediately, her fingers slipping up into the thickness of his hair and delighting in the vital feeling of it as it sprang back crisply against the back of her hand. "But you — Julio," she faltered, although now that she had got so far she had to go on, "you were very much in love with Gia's mother, weren't you?"

He put her away from him rather suddenly, and sat and looked at her.

"Who told you that?"

She was about to say, "Doña Beatriz" when he made it unnecessary for her to do so.

"My good friend Doña Beatriz de Camponelli has been putting in rather a lot of work on my behalf — or, rather, *against* me, I should say!" with a dryness that made her feel secretly glad she was not Doña Beatriz de Camponelli. "Lisa, I'll have to tell you the whole story about her, and about my wife, because otherwise there will always be doubts between us, and without complete faith there will never be complete accord."

He drew her back into his arms, and stroked her face gently. "Darling, if Beatriz has made you unhappy I can only say that I am so much more than sorry. You see, you and I were *meant* to love one another from the beginning, and I think she must have guessed it. She has always been my good friend — or so I have always believed her to be! — and it would be foolish of me to pretend that I didn't know she wanted to marry me; but as I have already told you I never had the smallest intention of marrying her. She is *not* the type of woman I would ever wish to spend my life with, but I was beginning to wonder — just when you made your impact on my life! — how I was going to convince her of that. You see, my darling, perhaps I have been a little weak, but she was good to Gia, and I thought she was a good friend, and a busy professional man doesn't have much time to cope with problems in his private life. Also Beatriz was a connection of my wife's, and that gave her some sort of a hold over us. And another excellent reason why she took such a proprietorial interest in my affairs was because she knew how unhappy I had been, and what a failure my marriage was——"

"A *failure*?" Lisa interrupted him.

"Yes; a failure!" He looked a little grim. "You have talked to me more than once of arranged marriages, my dearest, and I told you that they were often a success, but that is not always so. My marriage was an arranged marriage — our families had been lifelong friends, and I don't suppose we would either of us have stood a chance if we'd tried to break away from what had been planned you might say in our cradles. And it was a bitter failure! My wife didn't really want marriage — she would have preferred a career. if she could have had one, and she didn't want children. When she knew that Gia was coming she did everything that might endanger her own life, as well as make it impossible for her to have the child, and within a week of the birth she took out her car and drove for so many miles that she exhausted herself and crashed into another vehicle, and when Gia was born she did die!" He looked away. "Not many Spanish women are like her, but then she was partly English."

"I am wholly English," Lisa reminded him in a whisper.

"Yes, but you are also my Lisa, my woman, and my love!" He looked down at her with a yearning tenderness that caused the color to fluctuate in her cheeks, and she made an impulsive movement towards him and clutched at him.

"Oh, Julio, if you really want to marry me I swear I'll think only of you, and make you happy! That is all I want to do!"

"I believe you, sweetheart." He carried her small hands up to his lips, and kissed the fingers of each one separately. "And you will also make Gia happy? Gia needs you, you know!"

"I know. And — Julio, you do love her, don't you?"

"I think I have loved her more since you came into our lives," he admitted, a little strangely. "You see, my marriage bewildered me, recoiled on me. Everything about it made me resentful, and I'm afraid I've allowed a certain amount of resentment to affect my attitude to Gia. But you can teach me to look upon her in a different light — you have already done that."

"You must love Gia," she whispered. "We will both love Gia!"

"And one of these days——" he began, but she colored so much that he refrained, and kissed her long and passionately instead.

Suddenly she realized that she hadn't even asked him how he had got there, and when he had arrived. When he admitted that he had followed her almost immediately and spent the night before at the local inn, because it had been too late to look her up in the cottage, the further realization struck home that it was so early that he probably hadn't had any breakfast.

"Food is unimportant when you're in love," he told her, a faint twinkle in his dark eyes. "And in any case, my dearest heart, I can never feel sufficiently grateful to a sleepless night that caused me to get up early and determine to start looking for you without delay, and by good luck I saw you as soon as you started down that cliff path."

"I think it was because I haven't had any breakfast either that I felt a bit dizzy," she explained. "I don't ever remember losing my nerve like that before."

He drew her to her feet.

"And how much food did you have yesterday?"

"I — I can't quite remember!" She dimpled suddenly, feeling so radiantly happy that everything had suddenly become a joke, a huge and glorious joke. "I think I opened one or two tins, but I don't remember sampling the contents. And Mrs. Pendenis's youngest was preoccupied with the dentist, so she couldn't come up to cook or do any cleaning."

Julio looked puzzled.

"I'll confess I can't see the connection between a Mrs. Pendenis — who sounds as if she might be some sort of a daily help! — her youngest's toothache, and your not sampling the contents of the tins you opened! But if this same daily help isn't due to arrive soon, don't you think we ought to go in and concoct something in the nature of breakfast for both of us? I presume, Miss Waring, that you can make coffee, if nothing else, and after that we can go to my inn and have breakfast."

"But that would make the villagers talk," she said, dimpling afresh. "No, Dr. Fernandez, *I* will cook breakfast — an English bacon and egg breakfast! — and we will both eat it, and then if Mrs. Pendenis doesn't arrive I'd better start tidying up the cottage." She looked up at it. "I thought it an ugly cottage when I arrived, but I don't think so now. I think," breathlessly, "that it's a lovely cottage!"

He looked up at it, too; and then he observed in a smooth tone, as he drew her close to him once more:

"Your friend Miss Tracey offered it to me as a honeymoon cottage, but I explained that I would have to take you straight back to Madrid, as there are a great many things there which I have to attend to during the next week or so. But the most important thing I have to attend to is to get you safely married to me, and after that we will be delighted to have her, and then go off somewhere where we can be really alone. . . ." He looked deep into her eyes, longingly, searchingly. "Do you yearn, as I do, for the moment when we will be really alone, and really the property of each other, my golden-headed Lisa?"

She put back that same golden head against his shoulder, and looked up at him.

"You know I do!" she said, so simply that he crushed his mouth hungrily against hers. And for fully another five minutes they forgot about breakfast, and Mrs. Pendennis, toiling up the hill from the village, wondered whether there was something wrong with her eyesight.

THE END